So Much Bad
In the
Best of Us

So Much Bad
In the
Best of Us

Cheryl Robillard

ISBN: 978-0-9977477-7-5

Library of Congress Control Number: 2019935033

Published by 102nd Place, LLC
        Scottsdale, AZ 85266

First Printing March, 2019

Printed in the United States

1
Little Lolo

My first memories are when I was around four years old, and all I knew is that I killed my mother. She died in childbirth. Okay, I know giving birth to me killed her, but I also wonder if she decided to die rather than be my mother. Or maybe she just couldn't get away from my father fast enough? No, I killed her for sure. My father told me so.

Miss Sarah told me that my mother couldn't wait to have a baby. She actually lost five other babies pretty early in the first or second trimester. One she had in the car on the way to the hospital and another she gave birth to while waiting in an emergency room for a doctor to show up. Those two were the hardest because they were perfectly formed boys, about 1 or 2 pounds. What kind of God lets this happen five times and then kills you?

Anyway, my mom was no quitter, and hope springs eternal for the optimist. Being a pessimist myself, I wouldn't know how to be a mother. I'd screw up another life for sure.

I guess it's the reason my father hated me and took to heavy drinking every night. There were strict orders to feed me and put me to bed before he got home around 8:00 pm. He'd come home already drunk and did not stop drinking until he passed out on the couch every night. He never slept in "their" bed again.

After he passed out, I would sometimes go downstairs and sit by him and just stare. I could only do it then because when he was awake, I was too afraid to look at him. Usually, I would pretend that we were having a conversation because in the morning we'd pass in the hall like strangers. Any words spoken were to my nanny, and he was usually trying to get her to take me home with her for the weekend. If no one would take me, he just left me with a box of cereal and a bowl.

One weekend, nothing was left out for me to eat. I finally worked up the courage to shake his arm and say, "Daddy, there's no cereal on the table."

He yelled, "Climb, Stupid. Climb!" and went back to sleep.

I got a kitchen chair and pushed it over to the cupboard and climbed up on the counter and reached for the box. It flipped off the shelf and spilled all over the floor. After I stomped around on it and ground it into the linoleum, I took the rest of the cereal in the box and went outside to play. I tipped over the chair for dramatic effect and left the mess for him to clean up.

My father was an imposing figure, big and tall. He was 6'4" and 240 pounds, all muscle from years of physical labor. He was a good-looking man with big steel blue eyes and a slick black pompadour. He did have rather bad skin though, with pockmarks and always a few pustules. I studied those nooks and crannies of his face with great interest.

His voice, like his skin, always seemed angry when he spoke, and I wondered if he sounded that way to my mother. I imagined he was soft and sweet to her. He called her Lovey.

Once he called me Lovey. He came home late and very drunk, bumping into things as he made his way into his bedroom where he got out of his work clothes. He staggered back to the living room in his undershirt and boxers and finally collapsed face first onto the couch. I watched from the top of the stairs. When I heard the familiar deep snoring snorts and I was sure he was fast asleep, I knew it was safe to go to him.

This time I curled up beside him and petted him like a sweet doggie. I could feel his hot breath coming faster against my hair. Then he threw his arm around me and called me Lovey.

At that moment, I felt certain that if he would get to know me, he would love me, and this was a start. I didn't push my luck though. When he shifted and moved his arm, I got up very quietly and tiptoed back to my room.

In the morning, I smiled when I saw him, but he was too busy to notice. No worries. I wasn't going to give up.

This became my ritual. Every night, I would wait until he passed out drunk, and then I'd go sit by my father. Sometimes, I'd whisper to him about my day or what Sarah and I had done. Sometimes I'd just imagine what it would be like if he woke up and said he loved me. And when I thought he was really sound asleep, I'd curl up next to him on the couch and hope he'd call me Lovey again.

Then one night, I must have misjudged something. When I cuddled in and wiggled closer, it woke the monster. His hand up my nightgown was rough and something mean between my legs was pushing, pushing into me.

"Ouch, ow, ow. Stop!" I pushed back and tried to get away, but I was trapped. It was a grunting, angry trap. Then it was like he saw me for the first time. He yelled, "You!"

"Yes, Daddy, it's me. I'm sorry." I begged for forgiveness.

He can't hear my cries because of the dark words that the monster yells. "You cunt. You fucking bitch." More grunts and then he let go. He pushed me to the floor where I lay like a half-dead fish.

I pretend I'm dead, afraid to even twitch for fear of what might happen next. Maybe my head may be cut off. After a few minutes, that seem like an eternity, he farts loudly and rolls over. The snoring begins again.

Eventually, I crawl to the stairs and try to make my shaking legs stand up. The pain between my thighs is raw and something is running down my leg. I wipe it with my nightgown and the blood terrifies me. It is thick and icky. Am I going to bleed to death? I get back to my room, weak and shivering and wait to die. What else can I do?

To my surprise, I wake up and it is morning. I survived the nightmare, but I know it was not a nightmare. It was real. My nightgown is stiff with smelly dried blood. I can't walk with my legs together and it hurts to pee. I bury my nightgown in the alley behind our house. I bury it deep, along with my fear and hatred.

.

2

Alleluia and Fried Chicken

My nanny's name was Sarah Johnson, but she is Miss Sarah to me. She was a sweet brown beauty. A loving Negro woman, who often held me to her ample breasts, and then scared the shit out of me with her stories about Jesus. She had me on my knees praying for forgiveness and salvation from the devil's work. Then, the next thing I knew we'd be singing "Jesus Loves Me." I couldn't figure out if he loved me or was going to smite me any minute. I was not really sure what smite was, but I figured it would hurt, so I should avoid it if at all possible. I knew I had to keep praying since I killed my mother, and that must be the biggest sin of all.

Still, some of my fondest memories are of standing on the red captain's chair beside the stove, watching Miss Sarah cook, while we sang Jesus songs and recited nursery rhymes. "Little Bo Peep, lost her sheep. Jack and Jill went up the hill." Sometimes we would play a game that I would make up, like jumping from a red square to a white square on our linoleum kitchen floor while she mopped behind me.

I loved the times I went home with her. There was always a flock of children in her yard, including her five and most of the kids from the neighborhood, and we all ran wild. We didn't have to come in and go to bed until dark, and we didn't even have to have a bath or get pajamas on. If we had our swimsuits on because we were running through the sprinkler or swimming in the pond behind the church, we'd be in those swimsuits for days, and we would sleep in them too. We smelled like dirty feet and pond scum. We smelled like summer. In the winter we would stay outside until we were half frozen, not wanting the fun to end. We smelled like mothballs and winter wool sweat.

At night all six of us slept in the same room, three boys in one bed and three girls in the other, telling stories until we fell asleep. Mostly we retold Bible stories that we had heard, but Tyrone would make up ghost stories, and Ruthie, Marilee and I would end up praying to Jesus to save us. "If we should die before we wake, we pray the Lord our soul to take." The other possibility was even scarier. The devil might come and snatch us up during the middle of the night if we'd been bad, and we always believed we'd been bad.

There was a story Tyrone liked to tell and we begged to hear, even though it usually made someone wet the bed. It went like this:

Now this here's a true story, swear to God. (That's how he always started the story) *There was a girl who had a new dress, and she wanted to go to the dance on a Saturday night, but her Mama say no. "No way you gonna go to town, 'cuz you too young and they be bad men hangin' around juz waitin fo a pretty young thing who is too stupid to stay home where she belong with her Mama." That's what her Mama say, but this girl made up her mind she gonna go. She don't think her Mama know nothin and don't want her to have no fun.*

So, she wait til her Mama's sleepin good. Then she put on her new dress and sneak out of the house and down to the town where the music was playin and folks was dancin and laughin. Well, she was havin a good time when a tall, handsome man come in. He was so fine lookin, all dressed real good, black hair, and blue eyes shinin. All the girls were bout to faint cuz he so good lookin and he look like he got lots o' money too. But he walk right up to our girl and he say "May I have this dance?"

Well, our girl think she done gone to heaven and they start dancin. Everyone else stop dancin and juz watchin them. He spinnin and twirlin her around the floor real nice, but then he start goin faster and faster and then two horns pop right out of his head and he grow'd a tail comin right outta his pants. He still spinnin her faster and faster and then his feet turned into hooves and he spun her right out the door. And nobody ever seen her again"

"What color was the girl?" Ruthie, asked.

"Why she white, of course. Dose white gals, they neva mind they mamas." I feel Tyrone looking at me in the dark

"And what color the devil be?" Ruthie persists.

"Why, he be white too. White devil, thaz what." I think Tyrone is teasing me now, cuz everybody knows the devil is red. Besides, Tyrone is always teasing me.

We could hardly catch our breath after that because we felt a little guilty. I'll just say there were some curious kids checking out to see if there was any difference between colored girls and white girls. And guess what – no difference.

My other concern was that the devil in the story sounded just like my father. But mostly when I was with the Johnsons, I felt safe because I was with my family. They were my family and aren't families the best? I finally had one. I was a Johnson now. I knew what it was like to belong.

Belonging to a family with boys was an education in itself. I saw my first penis at Miss Sarah's one night when I walked in on Tyrone going to the bathroom. I just froze and stared in amazement. He saw me but made no attempt to hide anything. In fact, he jiggled it around for a pretty long time and he watched my face as he did it. I didn't make any attempt to run away, so I guess we both were amazed. Finally, he put it away and walked past me without a word. After that, we looked at each other differently. We shared a secret, and I figured he must be my boyfriend.

Sunday morning was a different story. We had to wash our face and hands and get clean clothes on, including shoes. All spit-shined for Jesus. I would be the only white face in a sea of black and brown, but it didn't matter to anyone. I sang the hymns loud and proud, and when some folks took to dancing in the aisle, I was right there with 'em. I took great glory in raising my arms up to heaven and shouting "Hallelujah" and "Praise Jesus." Miss Sarah would tell me to shush, but Lord, the Spirit moved me on those Sundays.

All smiles and feeling good from all the singing and shaking hands, we paraded down the street to Miss Sarah's house. Miss Sarah's husband, Luke, would be out on the front porch waiting for her with a cold beer. They would sit together and talk and laugh loudly.

People passing by would yell, "How you doin?" or "Lovely mornin, ain't it?" Some would stop and chat for a while, mostly to gossip about who was sick or in jail or run off. We girls would sit on the broken-down steps of the porch and not say a word, but just listen to the adults and try to learn how to be just like them. The boys would be out back shooting hoops or doing something fun that they would never let us girls get in on.

About two in the afternoon, Miss Sarah would make a batch of fried chicken and mashed potatoes that I loved. There was also some kind of greens that I didn't love and didn't eat. Miss Sarah never made me eat anything I didn't like. Instead, she'd fix me an extra biscuit with honey. That's what a Mother does for her baby.

3

Everybody Knows but Me

I hated the idea of going to school even though Miss Sarah told me it was going to be lots of fun with toys and other kids to play with. In reality, it was nothing like that. There was a mean boy who pinched me every chance he got, and the girls wouldn't let me play in the playhouse with them. They said there wasn't room, but there was. The teacher didn't make them be nice to me either. Instead, she put an apron on me and I had to paint something with some crappy paint that ran instead of staying where I put it. Thanks a lot for one more thing for the other kids to laugh at.

I felt like everyone knew what was going on but me. Probably my father knew but didn't tell me. I was now beginning to have serious doubts about him.

"So, you say you don't like your little daughter. Well, guess what, Mister. She doesn't like you either."

What a relief when the stupid bell would ring and I could leave school. Miss Sarah would be waiting outside and we would walk home together.

"How was school, Lolo?" She called me Lolo, not Loretta, and I wished everyone would.

"It was fine, Miss Sarah, but I like being with you better. Do I have to go back?"

"Yez, you gots to go back. It be the law, honey. Anyways, you gots to go to school to be smart. World don like no stupid people."

"But I ain't learnin nothin. Stupid songs like the 'Wheels on the Bus Go Round and Round.' How else they gonna go?"

Miss Sarah laughed at that. I loved to hear her laugh. Wish I knew what I said that was so funny though.

"Lolo, you ain't suppose to say ain't. That's learnin, that be smart. Okay?"

"But you say ain't and you," I searched for the correct word, "not stupid."

"You just pay mind to yo schoolin, Lolo. You be smarter than me or you be babysittin and cleanin toilets fo a livin. Got it?"

"Yes, Miss Sarah. Let's sing *This Little Light of Mine.*"

Through the years, I tried my best to do what Miss Sarah said, but it just didn't seem that easy to make friends or to do very good at my lessons. Or is that supposed to be "very well?" See, I'm still not good or well at it.

When report card time came, I tried to make my D's into B's so my father wouldn't know how dumb I was. I didn't understand that he didn't care what I did in or out of school as long as I didn't bother him.

If I didn't go home with Miss Sarah for the weekend, I would entertain myself by walking downtown where we had two movie theaters. Sounds kind of crazy but the good thing was, they were across the street from each other. On Saturday they both had double features and a serial short that ended in a cliffhanger. Even though I went almost every Saturday, I never got to see how the cliffhanger got resolved. There would just be another short with another cliffhanger. It really made me mad, but what could I do? It was much better when there was an old episode of *Our Gang.*

I would change my mind about what I wanted to be when I grew up depending on what the movie heroine was up to. After *Florence Nightingale*, I wanted to be a nurse. Other times I wanted to swim the English Channel or be a showgirl, a dancer, a cowgirl, a movie star or a mother with 12 children. I thought there were so many wonderful choices, but what did I know? How would I ever choose just one?

Miss Sarah and I didn't go to my father's business very often, but when we did, I had to stay out in the front or in the back where the workmen were. Luke, Sarah's husband, was usually back there, and he was really nice and always had gum. The guys treated me just like one of them and they laughed when I said stuff like "when is that fucking rock going to be delivered?" I said it every time and it always got a laugh.

I liked listening to them talk about the jobs they were doing. It sounded like they were having fun and making concrete and sidewalks and something called slabs. They called my dad "The Boss" and they called me "Little Boss" sometimes. I think I'd like to work there when I grow up . . . if I don't become a movie star.

When the guys were out on a job, I just sat in a chair in the front and watched my father and Miss Sarah through the glass door to his office. It looks like it is good to be "The Boss." He owns the building and gets to tell everyone what to do. Sometimes people come in to see him, but they have to wait in line. I can tell he's an important man.

One particular day was special because now there was a lady sitting at a desk outside of my father's office. She was the most beautiful lady I had ever seen in person. She had red hair and red nail polish and red lipstick. She was wearing a pink sweater and a tight black skirt with real high heels. She looked like a girl on a calendar and she gave me a big smile.

"I'm Loretta, who are you?"

"My name is Margaret, and I'm your father's secretary."

I could tell we were going to be good friends because she talked real sweet to me, and when I asked her if she liked movies she said she did.

"I love movies! What is your favorite?" Margaret asked.

"I like any musical. I want to be in the movies and dance like this." I then did my best tap impression and she actually clapped.

"You can call me Lolo. That's what all my friends call me."

"And you can call me Maggie. That's what *all my friends call me*." And then she laughed. It was a real nice laugh. I practiced imitating it all day.

"Hey, we should go to the movies together. There's a double feature on Saturday do you want to go then?" About that time Miss Sarah came out of my father's office, grabbed my hand, and pulled me out the door before Maggie could answer.

"Call me," I yelled over my shoulder.

4

A Pig's Tail/Tale

Something happened at school that was blown way out of proportion by stupid, fat ass Alice Fairfield. Or as I called her, Alice Fartfield. She started it by hitting me in the head with a dodgeball, and I wasn't even playing dodgeball. So, I called her a name and gave her a little shove. It's not my fault that she has no balance and fell on her fat ass. Then she began to wail her head off and tattled to the playground teacher on duty who, by the way, has had it in for me since kindergarten.

The next thing I know, I'm hauled into the Principal's office and told to sit in the corner. "You'll be dealt with later," he says. Then, holy crap here comes my father and Miss Sarah. My father's face is twisted into a scary scowl, and he gives me the evil eye.

In Mr. Sybley's office, the story is told in a totally one-sided way, and I am not allowed to tell my side at all. I'm thinking this will all blow over now, and I can get on with my shitty life, but no such luck. Mr. Sybley says the major offense is the name I called Fat Ass; I mean Alice. Seems 'fat fucking cunt' is a big deal. Mr. Sybley actually wrote it out and showed it to my father instead of repeating it. He said this language could not be tolerated and I was expelled.

My thought was, "At last, something good has happened, and

it was totally worth getting hit in the head." I thought I didn't have to go back to school, ever.

"Thank you, Mr. Sybley. I will take care of this, and I apologize for any embarrassment," my father said, as he grabbed me by my collar and ushered me out the door with such force that my feet were barely touching the ground.

When we got to the street, he looked at Miss Sarah and through clenched teeth, he said, "You are fired. You are never to speak to Loretta again. Do you understand?"

"Why? Mr. Nelson, you don't think I taught her that kind of talk?"

"Yes, I do. You or Luke, or one of your filthy boys. Your paycheck will be mailed to you. Now leave."

"What? NO! NO! You can't fire her. I want her. She's my MOTHER! Miss Sarah, don't go, don't go, don't go." I hung on to her for dear life.

She hugged me hard, and then held me at arms' length, looked me in the eyes and said, "One day someone will hug you so tight that all of your broken pieces will fit back together."

We both were in tears as my father pulled us apart before I could ask her "what the hell does that mean?"

"Bye, Lolo," she mouthed.

My father picked me up and tossed me into the back of his car. "No, no." I watched Sarah standing there waving at me as we drove away. I was getting hysterical as the shock of what just happened began to sink in. I began kicking the back of his seat and screaming.

"Shut up, or I'll give you something to cry about," he yelled.

He wasn't one for idle threats so I gulped my cries and shed my silent tears. As we pulled into our dark garage, I sensed the danger that awaited me. I could smell it in the air. I cowered in the corner of the back seat.

In an instant, the situation went from bad to brutal. The car door flew open, and he grabbed me by the leg and pulled me across the seat. In an instant, he was on top of me. My skirt was pulled up and he held me down by my pigtail. I braced myself for what was coming. I was powerless, vulnerable. No one could save me. It was useless to struggle.

I wanted to call him a fat fucking cunt, just like he had called me a hundred times. Instead, I just repeated the thought, "I hate you and I hope you die."

When it was over, I ran to my room and waited. I am repulsed by the familiar smell and guck he has left on me. When I am certain he is asleep, I take my revenge with the only power I have. In the kitchen, I retrieve the scissors Miss Sarah kept in the sewing drawer. I walk back into the living room with the intent and purpose of a military commander. For an instant, I think about stabbing him in his eye or maybe his heart, but I doubt he has one. I stand over his body on the couch, listening to his nasal breathing.

Taking the scissors in my right hand, and holding one of my pigtails with my left hand, I hacked through the thick braid until it came off in my hand. I dropped it on the floor beside him and continued with the other one. There is nothing he can ever do to me again. I doubled down on my self-inflicted wounds.

5

I Don't Want Nun

The next morning when I woke up, he and the pigtails were already gone. I didn't know what would happen next. Did this mean I never had to go to school again? If I would have known this before, I would have called everyone at school any number of the names my father had used on me. Lord knows there were plenty to choose from.

While I was enjoying my freedom and a grape Popsicle for breakfast, I turned on the radio and marched gingerly around the breakfast table with Don McNeil's Breakfast Club.

Someone knocked at the front door, and for a second, I thought it might be Miss Sarah, but she didn't ever knock. I hesitated to open it, fearing it might be the dreaded truant officer I had been warned about but didn't believe existed. I was in no mood to be dragged back to school, but just in case it was Miss Sarah, I had to open it. I was sure she couldn't be gone forever.

Instead, when I opened the door, I saw my father's secretary. I don't know who was the most shocked – me to see Margaret standing there, or Margaret looking at my new haircut, swollen red eyes and purple lips.

"Good morning, Loretta, May I come in?"

"Yes, of course, come in. Would you like a Popsicle?"

"No thank you, honey. I'm actually here to get you ready to go to Blessed Sacrament so we can get you registered for your new school," she said. "Can you dress yourself or would you like me to help you?"

Oh, crap. A new school. "No, I can do it."

I reluctantly went to my room to get dressed. I decided to wear my favorite outfit – one that I hardly ever got to wear otherwise. Miss Sarah didn't want to buy it for me that day at Sears, saying it wasn't practical. But I had insisted, declaring it was the only thing in the world that I wanted, so she finally relented.

"I don know what yo daddy gonna say bout this, but go ahead and try it on."

It had a navy-blue taffeta skirt with pink crinolines, topped off with a sheer blouse adorned with pink fuzzy polka dots and puffy sleeves. It made me feel like Shirley Temple when I put it on.

Turns out Miss Sarah was right. It wasn't practical for school and playing on the jungle gym or playing kickball, but it was perfect for making a grand entrance at my new school. If I had to do this, at least I was going to do it in my own style.

When I came down the stairs Margaret stared at me and didn't say anything at first. I was pretty sure the beauty of my outfit took her breath away.

"Dahling!" I gave a twirl and said, "What do ya think?" Before she could comment, I said, "Oh, wait till I put on my new Mary Jane's with the cleats."

The cleats were another one of my great ideas that Miss Sarah joyfully went along with. Actually, I wanted taps but settled for cleats. I put them on and did my version of a tap dance for Margaret.

Slightly out of breath, I asked, "Do I look like Shirley

Temple?" And gave a little curtsy. All this took a great deal of effort due to the stinging raw wound between my legs.

Margaret gave me a big smile and said "Well, ah, yes, you do! I guess you are ready to go." I could tell I had really impressed her.

Margaret and I walked to the new school. It was only eight blocks away, but she wanted me to know how to get there on my own. The day was gloomy, and the wind whipped around my anklets and stung my bare legs. I focused on my best tap dance instead of just a plain old walking step to keep from thinking about yesterday or worrying about the new school of torture that loomed before me. Click, click, and click, on the brick sidewalk.

"Do I have to stay there all day or are we just registering, and then we can leave and maybe go to a movie?"

"I'm not sure what will happen, Loretta, but I'm sure there won't be a movie. I have to get back to work, but if you stay or not, I will be here to walk you back home. So, don't worry about that."

I was aware of her effort to put this in a good light. I felt she understood what I was going through even though we didn't talk about it. I took her hand and continued to tap. All too soon we were standing in front of Blessed Sacrament, and I stopped in my tracks, unable or unwilling to make my body go up the steps. I don't actually remember how I navigated the steps but somehow I found myself inside.

The school was enormous, and I was afraid I would never find my way around. I imagined being lost for days, and finally being found in the corner of some vast room, dead from starvation. Of course, I was wearing my beautiful outfit with my hair looking lovely because it would have grown out by then, and I would have a blissful half smile on my angelic dead face.

"What a tragedy . . . She was so talented, and now the world will never know . . . She was so sweet. Why didn't we pay more attention to her when she was alive?" People would be saying all these wonderful things about me and feeling guilty that they were so mean to me. There would even be a full-page write-up in the *Rockton Republic* about my demonic father and my short tragic life.

My daydream was interrupted by Sister Mary Magdalene, storming down the hall straight at me like a black tornado. She walked with the stride of a racehorse. Those long rosary beads were swinging and clanging with each galloping step. Her face was reddish, and it looked like her head was wrapped too tight in some sort of stiff, white cloth and her face might pop at any minute. She was not a woman to mess with. That was obvious.

We followed her into her office, and the inquisition began. After the usual questions about my family history, age, and previous education, she came to the real nitty-gritty.

"Religion?" she asked

Margaret looked at me for the answer. I searched my brain, and finally blurted out, "The Negro Church by Miss Sarah's."

They both looked at me like Luke's dog Skippy did when I told him to roll over. I realized they needed more information, so I explained. "The one where Jesus will damn you to hell if you drink too much and fornicate." I added, "Like my dad."

I was escorted to a bench outside in the hall while the adults made the decision that I would become a Catholic.

While I was waiting, a vision in black floated towards me. She stopped in front of me, smiled, and held out her hand. I took it like I was in a trance. My eyes never left her soft blue eyes for a second.

"Good morning, Loretta. My name is Sister Mary Theresa and I will be your teacher this year. You may just call me

Sister," she said, in a voice that sounded like birds singing.

She held my hand as we walked down the hall to her classroom. I tried to keep my cleats from making that clicking noise, but the sound echoed like thunder on the well-polished floors, bouncing off the walls and into my ears with each step.

"What kind of floors are these?" I asked in search of something to divert her attention from the noise.

"Terrazzo" she replied. I didn't know what to do with that information, but I faked it, saying "Oh, I'll have to tell my father to get some like that for his office."

Finally, we entered her classroom. She introduced me to the class as she walked me to an empty desk. Click, click, click.

"Class, this is Loretta. She will be depending on each one of you to show her around until she is familiar with everything. Be nice and remember what it was like when you were the new student."

I took a seat and felt very self-consciously over-dressed. Every other girl had on the identical blue pleated skirt, white blouse, navy blue knee socks, and brown oxfords. I could see them rolling their eyes at each other and stifling giggles.

Thankfully, recess was already over, and all I had to get through was lunch. When the lunch bell rang, all the children scattered. I just sat at my desk waiting for death or some excuse to make me disappear. I was wondering if I could make a run for it when Sister came over and said, "Come this way, Loretta. I will show you where the lunchroom is, and where the girls' bathroom is located."

Click, click, click. I left the lunchroom as soon as she walked away, and I went immediately to the girls' bathroom and stayed there until the end of lunch and the bell rang. Then I hurried to my desk before anyone could hear or see me.

6

Halo, Everybody, Halo

At three o'clock I followed the crowd out the front door, and there was Margaret sitting on the stoop, smoking a cigarette. I ran to her and hoped my classmates would see me with her and think that she was my beautiful mother.

"Hi, Lolo. How was your first day?" she asked as she flipped her cigarette into the street.

"Horrible, the worst day of my life, and I'm not making that up!" I started to cry, but I didn't want her to think that I was a baby, so I just kept up a steady stream of demands instead.

"I need that outfit the other girls are wearing and new shoes, and I want a 'Toni' home perm and some Halo Shampoo."

I had seen an ad in the magazine for Halo shampoo, and I was certain that was all I needed to be transformed into the girl in the picture or the girl on the Toni perm box.

Margaret took me shopping, and we got everything on my list. I sat at the counter of Woolworth's and ate a hamburger and potato chips while she bought the shampoo and perm.

Then she took me to her house, and she and her aunt gave me a haircut, and the permanent, and washed my hair in Halo shampoo. After all this, I couldn't wait to see how beautiful I was.

Margaret handed me a mirror. Holy Shit! This just wasn't my

day. I didn't look anything like those girls in the magazine or on the Toni box. It was more like Buckwheat.

I was positive it was all Margaret's fault. She must have done it all wrong. I admit I went a little crazy but who could blame me? I burst out crying and began screaming.

"Moron! Stupid, stupid asshole! Idiot." The words poured out, and very soon they were just a mixture of snot and sobs and high-pitched hissing sounds. I picked up the shampoo and threw it at her. The cap was not on tight and shampoo went everywhere. They just stared at me in astonishment as I stomped around their kitchen.

Out of the blue, Margaret's uncle grabbed me and began shaking me. "Stop it! Stop it, right now, young lady."

Startled and literally shook up, I did stop. He put me down and walked away. Margaret packed up all my stuff and we drove home in silence.

Once inside my house, I ran up to my room and cried myself to sleep for the second night in a row.

The next morning, I got dressed in my new school uniform. I tried brushing through my rat nest of hair, but it was no use, so I retrieved a knit cap from the front hall closet. I would think of a good reason to tell Sister why I had to keep it on all the time. At any rate, I was determined to wear it until my hair grew out.

I ate my Rice Krispies in bitter silence while I plotted my revenge. *Snap, Crackle, Pop.*

To my surprise, Margaret had the nerve to show up to walk me to school. "Good morning, Loretta."

"I'm not taking the hat off so tell Sister to get used to it."

We walked to school without any discussion of the debacle last night. I'm sure she wanted to apologize but didn't know how. She tried to make small talk, but I was going to make her suffer for what she did. I pretended to be totally focused on unraveling a thread of my mitten. By the time we got to school, I had a nice ball of yarn. I put it in my pocket and squeezed it for courage. I kept my eyes down as I walked past Sister.

"Loretta?" Sister started to say something to me, but I walked faster to my desk. She and Margaret spoke in low voices and then Margaret left. Nothing more was ever said about my hat.

The recess bell rang, and I lingered at my desk, pretending to be looking for something inside. I thought maybe I could just keep looking until recess was over, but then I heard Sister's footsteps coming and stopping beside me.

"Loretta?"

"Oh, um, hi. Hello, Sister."

She bent down so we were face-to-face, and said, "Loretta, the correct way to greet me is to say, 'Good morning, Sister.' Do you understand?"

I stared into her mouth at her overbite as she spoke. She reminded me of Gene Tierney without makeup. She would definitely look better with some lipstick.

"Yes, Good morning, Sister," I said with my sweetest smile.

"Lovely to see you today, Loretta." She said and patted me on the arm. "If you are not feeling well enough to go outside, you can stay at your desk and color."

I quickly figured out the hat story meant I was dealing with some sort of illness, so I conjured up my weakest voice and sick puppy face. "Thank you, Sister. I would just like to put my head down and rest." I used the time to daydream.

I spent lunch hour in the bathroom and afternoon recess resting at my desk again. Finally, the school bell rang, and I could get out of that hell hole. I expected to see Margaret waiting for me outside, but she was not there.

When I got home, I found my Mary Jane's waiting for me on

the kitchen table. They had new taps on them with a note from Margaret that said, "When you have a bad hair day, just keep dancing."

All was forgiven and it turned out to be a pretty good day after all. I put on my new tap shoes, tapped all the way to the five-and-dime, bought a Little Lulu comic book and a Mars bar and stole a red lipstick.

7

Liar, Liar; Pants on Fire!

Back to reality and my stinking life. I sat at my desk with my hands folded like the other kids, trying to tell myself that everything was going to be okay. The class began with some prayers that I didn't know. I moved my lips like I did know what was going on, just in case anyone was watching me. I was pretty sure everyone was watching me. Again, everyone seemed to know what was going on except me.

I managed to get through most of the morning without incident until recess. I realized that couldn't fake illness or hide in the bathroom for the rest of my life so I might as well get on with it and venture out to the playground. I hovered close to the wall and watched the different groups to see where maybe I could fit in. The boys from my class were playing kickball while the girls were jumping rope. Another group of girls was playing jacks. That looked like something I could learn to do, and I didn't have to have a friend to do it with. Maybe I could just pretend that I enjoyed playing by myself. Now that I had a plan for recess, I could relax a little until lunch.

I decided I would just follow the girl who sat in front of me to the lunch room and do exactly as she did. I followed her through the lunch line and was thrilled to receive a grilled cheese sandwich and tomato soup, a carton of milk, and two

Graham crackers. Halleluiah, these Catholics really know how to eat!

I followed her to a table and sat at the end without making any eye contact so she wouldn't know I was tailing her. The other kids at the table were complaining about the Graham crackers for dessert.

I thought I might be invisible until some smart-ass boy named Paul said, "Hey, Fancy Pants. Where's your ballet outfit today?"

All eyes turned to me. I fought the instinct to jump up and punch him in his stupid face. Breathe. Count to ten like Miss Sarah says.

"Not that it's any of your beeswax, but the reason I was late and dressed like that is that I just flew in from California where I was auditioning for a movie."

The girl I followed in said, "Wow, did you get the job? Are you going to be a movie star?"

"Well, they want me, but my father thinks California isn't safe. You know, the Japs could send a submarine over and kill everyone," I said. "But my mother thinks I should do it, so we'll see."

Just that fast, I had a crowd around me firing questions. "Did you see any movie stars while you were there? Does California really have palm trees? What is Hollywood really like?" Blah, blah, blah. Fortunately, my obsession with movie magazines was now paying off. I name-dropped all the places I had read about until the bell rang, and we had to go to class, but my little white lie solidified my popularity for the rest of the week.

At recess, Paul passed me a note asking me to meet him in the alley for a kiss. Of course, I did and since it wasn't my first kiss. I mean it *was* my first real kiss with a real boy, but I had practiced on my arm, imitating the people in the movies. So, I knew a thing or two and that also added to my fame and reputation.

8
Sandy Box

Ever since I first met Margaret at my father's office, I have made beauty my life-long pursuit. I have spent hours studying movie magazines looking for beauty tips. Other girls waste their time playing with dolls or finger paints, while I am mastering the art of makeup and of being a sex symbol. I know what boys like.

I discovered how versatile a tube of lipstick could be. Not only did it give a little color to the lips if used lightly, but if dabbed on the cheeks and rubbed in, it gave a healthy glow to the skin. It was just as good as rouge, and who needs to spend money on two things when one will work. I never went to school without doing my makeup. I felt it was only expected from a soon-to-be a movie star.

One afternoon while walking home from school, I was followed by two twin girls that I recognized from my school, but they were two grades ahead of me. At some point, they caught up with me, and the bigger of the two began to push me around. She said, "You're not fooling anyone. We know you are wearing makeup. Who do you think you are? Hedy Lamar?" Then she slapped me across the face. I took off running. They chased me all the way home.

My long walk home every day after school became a journey

filled with peril at every turn. Should I linger, and hope they would go ahead? But then they could lay in wait for me. Or should I make a run for it? Should I take the alternate route with the snarling, barking bulldog blocking the sidewalk? I imagine his evil red eyes fixed on me and frothing saliva dripping from his fangs. Margaret and my father have no clue what my life is like. Between this and long division I may not make it through the year.

Then one day, I was outside on my porch playing jacks when I saw the smaller of the twins across the street playing with a cat. Divide and conquer – just the opportunity I needed.

"Hey is that your cat?" I yelled. "Can I see it?"

"Sure." She said, "but it's not my cat."

I walked over, sat down beside her on the grass and petted the cat.

"Whose cat is this?"

"I don't know. He just showed up."

"Let's keep him just for us. Okay?"

"Yes! What should we name him?"

"What is your name? Mine is Loretta, but you can call me Lolo."

"My name is Sandy Boxer."

"Great. Let's call him 'Boxer' because he looks like a good fighter." I smile at her. "Hey, do you want to play?" I asked. "I have jacks."

"Okay, I love jacks," she said

"All right, Sandy Box, let's go." She giggled at my joke and I knew we would be good friends from then on. I would never have to worry about walking home from school again.

We walked over to my porch and played jacks and talked. I found out Sandy lived across the street and down the block in an apartment with her twin sister, Patty, and her mom and dad.

Even though she was two years older than me, she was sort of young for her age, and I was rather old for my age, and we both had an adventurous spirit, so it was the perfect match. She was also easily led, and I liked that about her.

After we had played for about an hour, I decided it would be more fun if we played with a larger ball and more jacks than just ten. So, I suggested that we go to the five-and-dime and get more supplies. She wholeheartedly agreed that it was an excellent idea. I liked her already for her common sense.

I took her into my house and showed her my dad's bedroom, and the dresser where he always left change. I took a quarter, and we went on our first adventure, which involved walking six blocks, then maneuvering over a railroad trestle crossing, a major road, and another three blocks to get to the store. We took our time selecting our perfect ball and multicolored jacks and picking out a stash of candy.

I think everything would have worked out fine except we misjudged how long all of this would take. By the time we got back, it was close to supper time, and Sandy's mom was fit to be tied. Then when she found out where we had been, I thought she was going to faint. Sandy was grounded for a week and told she could never do that again.

Of course, we were found out because we never thought of a cover story for how and where we got the jacks. Another pattern – forgetting to plan the alibi, cover our tracks and think out all the angles. Ready, fire, aim: that was our motto if we had one.

I was mystified by what a big deal this was. Geez, you'd think we were babies who didn't know how to walk or cross a street. No one was going to tell me I couldn't. The question wasn't who's going to let me. It was who's going to stop me? I could see I would need to teach Sandy how to spare her mother the worrisome truth. Sometimes a lie is the kindest thing to do, for all concerned.

After Sandy was released from her prison, we were inseparable. Jacks, hopscotch, coloring books, hide and go seek, and paper dolls. We never ran out of ideas. Once in a while, I included Patty if we needed a third, or of course when I was invited to stay overnight. Sometimes, we played blind man's bluff in their little bedroom with the lights off. The laughter was intense and I'm sure there was a little pee in every corner.

However, Patty was such a goody-two-shoes and tattle tale that I didn't encourage a threesome unless absolutely necessary. I think anyone who cannot tell a lie is not trustworthy. But I have to admit that she did teach Sandy and me how to stand on our heads, do cartwheels, and backbends. From that moment on, we usually used these activities as our mode of transportation. I could walk on my hands for blocks and usually preferred the view of the world upside down. And I demanded Sandy follow my lead.

I knew I was the leader of our little gang with the best ideas, and I could always come up with the money, but being friends with them had advantages also. Spending the night away from my house and being fed homemade meals was like Christmas, or so I would guess. We didn't have Christmas at my house, but I heard from other kids that it is fun. I heard my father say there was no Santa Claus before I was in kindergarten when I wanted to go to the Christmas parade. It was the first I'd heard of Santa.

Miss Sarah didn't say either way, but Santa always left presents at her house for me. I think Santa didn't want to come to my house because he was scared off by my father. Who could blame him?

I liked it when Mrs. Boxer asked me to stay for lunch. She

made really good grilled cheese and or peanut butter and jelly sandwiches, and always included potato chips. I brought her a can of Hershey chocolate syrup so she could make us chocolate milk with our sandwiches.

Two weeks after Miss Sarah got fired, our house was a mess with dirty dishes, dirty clothes, and no food in the refrigerator. Then on a Wednesday when I came home from school, the house was clean. I had clean underwear, and everything was neatly put away in my dresser. There was cold fried chicken and spaghetti in the fridge and a chocolate cake on the counter. Fresh bread and baloney, too. Everything was just like it was when Miss Sarah was here. Every Wednesday after that it was the same thing.

On Wednesday morning before I left for school, I would sometimes leave a note:

Dear fairy godmother, thank you for the food and the cake. Please get corn flakes. And I need grape popsicles. I have some dresses on my bed for you if you have a little girl who wood like them. luve, Lolo

I would hurry home from school to see if there was a reply, but there never was. However, my wish list was always fulfilled, and the dresses were gone.

Back at school, now that I had an older friend to hang around with, my popularity points were multiplying, or so I imagined. My skills at multiplication were not. I felt like I didn't have a firm grasp on subtraction yet, and now I had to deal with this and long division. Again, everyone else seemed to be fine with it. It was only 1's and 2's and it scared me to realize it was just going to get harder. Sometimes I felt a lot smarter than everyone, and then stuff like this would happen, and I felt like I must be stupid. I thought it best not to dwell on it, or on my time's tables. UGHHHH, 1 x 1 =1? Seems like it should be 2. Who makes up this stuff anyway? I doubt I will ever need to know any of this.

9

Red Rider

Sandy and I played, sang, smoked cigarettes and stole from the five-and-dime. We also experimented with my dad's whiskey, but only once. After one gulp Sandy ended up gasping for breath on the floor, flopping around like a fish out of water. It scared the crap out of me, and I didn't push her to do that again. She needed to trust me since she was becoming quite the protégé under my tutelage.

The telephone was also a great form of entertainment. We took turns random dialing. When someone answered, we'd say, "Hello, this is "Name that Singer!" Then one of us would sing *"Your cheatin' heart will tell on yoooou."* It is surprising how many people guessed Patti Page instead of Hank Williams. We would be rolling on the floor in laughter and hang up, unable to tell them what their prize was.

Sandy's mother was always trying to engage us in more productive activities like cooking and baking, which I really did enjoy, and I became quite good at it. My specialty was hot dogs. I liked them split and then fried in butter until they were black and blistered. When that was finished, I put a piece of bread in the pan and fried it until all the butter was gone and it was dark and crusty. Yummy! Sandy liked it that way too.

We would take our plate of goodies and sit in front of the

radio in the living room and listen to Helen Trent. At night, I liked The Lone Ranger and The Cisco Kid. I would ride my horse (the arm of the couch) away into some wild adventure where I was the hero and saved the day.

Mrs. Boxer also taught me how to make eggs. I practiced scrambled first, and then we moved on to the more sophisticated "over easy," which required a lot of finesse to crack the shell without getting eggshells in the mix. Then the ultimate challenge was flipping it over without massacring the yolk.

After mastering the egg recipes, it occurred to me that I might open a restaurant when I grew up. I thought that would be fun and I could eat whatever was left over. Sounded like a win, win to me.

Before we moved on to the next phase of cooking, Sandy and Patty each got a two-wheel bicycle for their birthday. The bikes were used, but they were the best birthday present ever. Once in a while, I got to practice on one, especially when Patty was having piano lessons, even though she left instructions for me to "keep my mitts off."

As soon as I had mastered this skill, I went straight to my father's office and told him I needed a two-wheeler for school purposes, and I needed it by tomorrow. Of course, I didn't actually tell him, but Margaret gave him the message. I thought I would get to go shopping that day, but no word came. Instead, after school the next day, I found a blue Schwinn waiting for me in the garage. That really made me mad because I wanted a red one. He just never could get anything right. *Hello people. Do I have to do everything?*

Oh well, I accepted it with my usual grace. When I showed it to Sandy and told her how I wanted a red bike and my stupid father got me a blue one, she said "What an asshole."

"I know! But what can I do?"

Sandy changed the subject. "I'm going to name my bike Red Rider."

"Okay then, mine is Blue Blaze." And we were off.

There was no time for cooking lessons after that. I told Mrs. Boxer that maybe we could still cook in the winter or on rainy days, but I only said that because I'm sure she was disappointed when I told her we didn't have time for any more lessons. Geez, adults require a lot of coddling.

For the next couple of years, Sandy and I were literally hell on wheels. The freedom, the mobility, the wind in my hair – it just didn't get any better than that . . . unless the bike was red.

The first holiday season after Sandy and I became friends, we began our new tradition; me at her house for Thanksgiving and Christmas dinner. It was really fun helping Mrs. Boxer fix the turkey and dressing at Thanksgiving. We peeled potatoes and helped make pies. After dinner, we all played Monopoly and then had turkey sandwiches. Mrs. Boxer always made a plate for my father who I said was working on some big job. Of course, I hid it in the back of the fridge and ate it myself the next day in my room. I was very thankful I didn't have to share.

On Christmas day, I charmed another invite for dinner and played with the girls' new paper dolls and colored in their new coloring books. Mr. Boxer asked me what I got for Christmas and I told him I got new clothes, which was just what I wanted. Every year it was the same answer to the same question. Only once did the Boxers ever try to get my father to join them in anything. I am not sure how that conversation went, but they never tried again. I would have just died of embarrassment if he had said yes.

10

Tiny Dancer

Winter is the worst time of year, even with all the excuses to eat food and have parties. After New Year's Eve and Valentine's Day, there's just nothing but cold dirty snow and gray miserable days. It gets dark way too early.

By the time Sandy and Patty were in the 8th grade, it was getting harder and harder to spend enough time with Sandy. They were into cheerleading and boys. And Mrs. Boxer had enrolled them in ballroom dancing classes. They wore the school colored ribbons on their jackets to show everyone that they were graduating and going to be in high school. Big deal. So, what. Who cares?

The truth was that I was green with envy over their 8th-grade boobs, their pubic hair, and their menstruation. I was happy that Sandy told me when it happened to her, and even showed me her Kotex. Not a used one, of course, although I was curious and would have liked to see what it looked like, too. She just showed me how to put it on, and how to use the sanitary belt to hold it in place. I couldn't wait for all these glorious adult things to be mine.

I could tell that I was losing my influence with Sandy, and I was desperate to get her back. I thought that when summer came, it would be different and Sandy and I would be thinking up fun stuff to do, even with boys. I was no stranger to boys and necking. Hell, I had my first kiss in the third grade.

Finally, Easter arrived and Blessed Sacrament was all decked out to celebrate the murder of Jesus. I couldn't wait! We had a week off of school and even though we had to go to Mass on Good Friday and make our Easter duty, the weather was warm and we were going on vacation. I was all set to have some serious fun with Sandy, but when we were walking home from the last day of school, the girls told me they were going on vacation to Florida to visit relatives. I asked if they thought I could go along because I had never been to Florida. Patty said she would ask, but doubted it because it would be too many people in the car and too expensive to feed me. I said, "I can get money." Anyway, it didn't happen and I couldn't believe my crappy luck.

I spent my week going to movies, doing a little shoplifting, and avoiding my father. I did buy myself some jelly beans and red nail polish. I painted my fingernails and toenails. They looked really good, and I wished my Sandy Box was there to see.

Mid-week I got a really bad toothache and I tried to ignore it by chewing my jelly beans on the other side, but by the first day of school, I told my father, through Margret, that I had to go to the dentist. Margaret said she would take me.

I asked her "When?"

"I'll let you know after I make the appointment," she said.

"Well, I guess I'm just supposed to suck it up until the pain reaches my brain and kills me. Take your time and I'll offer it up like Sister says. Suffering builds character. I'm on my way to Sainthood."

The day of the appointment, I waited on the corner for Sandy until I was going to be late for school. I figured maybe they were still in Florida, so I had to run by myself. The weather had turned cold again, and the sky was gray and cloudy. The weather matched my mood, and I should have worn a coat, not just my blazer.

The lunch bell rang but before I could make it to the cafeteria, Sister Theresa caught up with me in the hall, and said I was supposed to take the bus downtown, get off at Choate's Department store, and Margaret would be waiting out in front to take me to the dentist. Sister insisted on walking with me to the bus stop and waiting until I got on the bus.

As the bus pulled away, it started to sprinkle and I watched Sister running back to the school. She was surprisingly fast running in all that material. By the time the bus got to Choate's Department Store, it was pouring down rain. Almost everyone got off the bus, but I hesitated because I didn't see Margaret anywhere. I didn't have any money on me since I used my lunch money on bus fare, so I didn't want to take a chance at being stranded in the rain with no way of getting home. I stayed on the bus figuring it would take me back to the school, and then I could walk home. Hopefully, the rain would have stopped by then.

The bus seemed to be wandering all around the town. I had no idea where I was, but then I saw Miss Sarah's church. I jumped up and began pulling on the rope that rang the bell and told the bus driver to stop.

I got off the bus and ran all the way to Miss Sarah's house. I was so happy. I was lost, but now I am found! I ran up the steps and began to bang on the front door. No one answered. Oh no. No one is home. Now I am keenly aware of being soaking wet and freezing, and my tooth hurt like hell. I began to sob just as the front door opened and there stood Tyrone.

"What the heck? Lollipop, whacho doin here?"

I didn't answer. I just threw myself into his arms.

"Git in here girl. You all wet." He looked up and down the street to see if anyone had seen me, and then he shut the door.

He led me into the kitchen where there was a big pot of soup simmering on the stove and he brought me towels. My teeth were chattering as I told him how I got lost. He listened while he took my wet clothes off and wrapped me in the warm towel. He took another towel and dried my hair – roughly at first and then gently. His big hands rubbed me all over and I finally stopped shivering.

"Is Miss Sarah here?" I looked around realizing that we were alone.

"Naw, she workin. They won't be home 'til after da kids gits home from school.

"Why are you home?" I asked

"I's feelin poorly, but I'm good now." We both sat on the kitchen chairs and looked at each other.

Finally, I said, "I sure have missed ya'll."

"I know, we all miss you too. But specially me and Ma. We miss you all da time and I don't think I ever goin' to see yo funny face agin." He laughed.

"You think I look funny, Tyrone?" I made a face to make him laugh again, but he took my face in his hands and said, "I think you da prettiest girl in town."

Then he kissed me. A real movie star kiss. His lips were warm and soft. My stomach jumped into my heart and I felt light-headed like I might die right there. He stopped, and looked into my eyes and said: "Did you like that, Lollipop?"

"Yes! Yes, I did, Tyrone. Are you my boyfriend now? Do you love me?"

"Of course, I sure do love you and you are my girlfriend forever. Lez go in my bedroom and play like we be married already." He took my hand and led me away. Easily and effortlessly I floated along.

He stopped at Miss Sarah's room and got some scarves. "Here, let me fix you up like Salome."

My towel dropped and he tied a scarf around my waist like a skirt, and another around my chest like a halter. I was wishing I had breasts and hoped he wasn't disappointed that I didn't.

In his bedroom, he lay on the bed and said, "Dance for me, Salome. I is your King and it is my command."

"Wait a minute. I have to go get something." I remembered I had my tube of lipstick in my blazer pocket, so I retrieved it and made myself look beautiful with red lips and pink cheeks. I could tell he was shocked but pleased when I reappeared.

I began to dance for him. He clapped and encouraged me along, and as I danced closer to him, he reached out and grabbed the scarf around my waist. It came off easily and I stopped not knowing what to do next. He said "Keep dancin'. I likes to look atchew."

My head and body were spinning with delight knowing that I was adored. I took the scarf back and used it like a veil.

"Come here and lay beside your King and be my Queen."

We laid beside each other and kissed, and he touched me until my whole body began to quiver. I stroked his hard penis and felt it throb and release in my hand.

"Do you want to put your penis inside me?"

He gave me a strange look and then said, "No, Lollipop. You shouldn't do dat less you wants a baby."

Huh, who knew? It never gave me a baby before, but I didn't say anything.

We fell asleep for a short while and then he woke with a start.

"Come on Lollipop, let's git you cleaned up." He took me into the shower with him. He showed me how to wash him:

gently where his "ball sack" was, but harder, and faster up and down on his penis until he groaned and said it was clean now.

Then he soaped me up and washed me softly. His fingers caressed me between my legs and a shiver of ecstasy ran up my body. We dried off and he got one of my old dresses from a box under Miss Sarah's bed. It still fit perfectly. It was then that I knew for sure that it was Miss Sarah who was making the fried chicken every Wednesday. It was the most perfect day of my life.

When the kids came home from school, Tyrone and I were sitting at the kitchen table eating a bowl of soup. When Miss Sarah and Luke got home, we were all playing cards.

"Lolo, how'd you git here?" Miss Sarah asked.

I told her the story and she said how smart I was.

"Luke, you best be takin Lolo home or her daddy have a fit."

We hugged goodbye and my heart felt heavy in my chest. I did not want to leave. Besides now my tooth began to hurt again.

Luke drove me home and we talked about what I was up to, and how things were pretty good now that most people had jobs again. He said even most colored folks had some kind of job and enough to eat. He said most of the men in town were either broken up by the war or had moved up North to work on assembly lines making cars. He said he didn't want to move, and he felt blessed that he was working for my father and so were a lot of his friends because most businesses didn't want Negroes working for them. He said my father was a good man.

Shortly after I got home, the phone rang. It was Margaret having a hysterical fit. She said she had been standing inside the door of the department store waiting for me, and when I didn't show up, she thought she was going to be fired for losing me. She had called the school, and Sister said I had gotten on the bus, so then she thought I had been kidnapped. It was now 8 o'clock, and she was back at the office looking for my father to tell him the bad news.

That made me laugh. I told her where I had been, and I said it would be best if my father didn't know any of this. She was clearly relieved and agreed it would be our secret.

"I'll get you another appointment tomorrow," she said.

The moon was full that night and little did I know, there were more than a couple of secrets being kept.

11
Maybelline

The next morning, I couldn't wait to tell Sandy about my boy-friend and the kissing. I decided that she didn't need to know about anything else, even though I thought she would like the information about the ball sack. I decided I'd tell her when she needs to know or when she shares something big with me.

I waited at the corner and then I couldn't wait any longer so I ran to her house. There was a big sign on the front door that said "Polio Quarantine." I banged on the door and Mr. Boxer yelled through it, "Go away, Loretta."

I kept banging but no one answered. I ran back home and wrote a message to Sandy.

Dear Sandy,
What is going on? Why are you in qarenteen? Please write me back. Lolo

I taped it to her back window so that she could read it.

I went on to school, but between thinking about Tyrone and Sandy, I don't remember anything about that day. I know that kids were talking to me and wanting me to sit at their table for lunch, but nothing mattered without Sandy, not even a tooth-ache.

After my dentist appointment, I hurried back to Sandy's house. My note was still taped to the window, but there was no reply. I got back to school just as the bell rang and I had to get back to class. I told Sister that I wasn't feeling well, and I should go home and rest.

"I might be getting polio."

Sister wanted to call my father, so I told her the truth about Sandy, and how upset I was and that was why I was feeling sick.

She said she knew about the situation and that it would be better if I stayed in school to take my mind off it. I said okay and went out to the playground. Then I promptly left and went back to Sandy's. No note for me. I banged on the door in vain.

Back at my lonely house, I couldn't eat or play jacks or anything. I finally went to bed and turned on the radio. It was just noise to help me stop thinking. I had nightmares all night long. There were monsters with long noses like elephants surrounding my bed. I tried to make a run for it but I couldn't run. I was on all fours just pulling myself along on the ground like a slug. My legs were paralyzed like I had polio. I was relieved to finally wake up and see the sun begin to rise. The sky was pink. A good sign I thought.

I wrote Sandy another note:

"Dear Sandy, Please, come to the window or write something so I know you are ok. Lolo"

I went to tape my note to the window again and there it was…

"Lolo, my mother died. She went swimming in Florida and got polio. It went to her lungs and she died. Just like that. I think my father is moving us to Minnesota where my aunt

lives. I am crying all the time. I miss my mother. I will write to you when I am in Minnesota. I can't write anymore."

I didn't know what to do when I read this. She was like my mother too. I went over to my father's office instead of going to school. When I walked in, I saw Margaret sitting at her desk and I burst into tears.

"What's the matter, Lolo?"

The question made me cry even more. I couldn't answer her for the longest time and she just waited until I could talk. When I told her what happened, she didn't even have to think for a minute. She knew just what to do.

She said "Lolo, Honey, there isn't anything we can do except pray and try to comfort Sandy and Patty and Mr. Boxer too. We'll ask Sister to have everyone light a candle and maybe the other students could write notes to the girls. Meanwhile, why don't we shop for groceries and some games and things for the girls to do while they are in quarantine?" Maggie made everything better or at least bearable for now.

She went in and talked to my father and I saw him give her money and keys to his car. We left and went to the dime store first. She picked out coloring books and big boxes of crayons, puzzles, lots of comic books, and I insisted on several movie magazines. I knew the coloring books were too immature for them but I didn't want to embarrass Margaret. She took my cue and bought some romance magazines.

She also bought four little red plastic containers that said "Maybelline Mascara." In the car, I asked her what it was for. She took one out, opened it up and spit in it. Then she took the little brush and mixed her spit with the black hard mascara until it filled the brush. Then she showed me how she put it on her eyelashes to make them look thick and dark.

"Wow, what a wonderful thing! This must be what the movie stars use. Maggie, you look just like a movie star when you put it on." I knew I would need to get some the next time I was at the five and dime. "Can I have one of those?"

"Sure. Here. Don't tell your dad. Okay?"

"I never tell him anything."

Sandy also needed to know about this. I was excited to share the news and the other two mascaras. I almost forgot I was supposed to be grieving, but it came back quickly, and no amount of mascara could fix it.

Then we went to the Thrifty Drug Store and ordered malts and egg salad sandwiches. Margaret thumbed through the movie magazines while we ate. When we were finished eating, she lit up a Pall Mall, and I asked if I could have one. After a considerable stare, she gave me the pack. Before we left, she bought a carton of Pall Malls.

We stopped at the grocery store and bought lunch meats, cheese, eggs, bread, and milk. Last, we stopped at the bakery and bought cookies and a cake.

We dropped the groceries at their front door and told Mr. Boxer it was there. He said he was grateful, and I could hear his voice crack with emotion.

Back at my house, we wrapped all the presents in tissue paper so it would be fun for them to unwrap. I noticed that she didn't include the romance magazines or the mascara. I didn't question her about it, but I was beginning to see another side to her. I guess everyone has cracks. We took all the gifts back over again, and Margaret told Mr. Boxer through the door that we were leaving presents for the girls and if there were any other groceries that they wanted to just leave a note every morning and we would deliver whatever they needed. I could hear Mr. Boxer's sobs.

Margaret and I then drove to school and met with Sister and told her our ideas to help the Boxer family. Sister thanked us for being so thoughtful and kind. Then she scolded me for leaving school without permission. She didn't seem all that mad though. I did have to go back to class which I didn't think was fair because my mother just died. I offered it up.

The next day there were hundreds of handmade cards for the family, and a Mass that the whole school attended at 2:00 pm that day. All the candles were lit. I wished Sandy could see it for herself. I wrote her a long letter describing it all and left it with the dozens of other cards at their front door.

12

Bye, Bye, Love

We communicated this way for the next three weeks. The day the quarantine was lifted, their bags were packed and ready to go. Sandy came to my house early in the morning and I went to the door in my PJ's. I was so happy to see her. I jumped in her arms up and down and squealed like a pig. We hugged and hugged and then she said she was leaving.

"Leaving? What do you mean, leaving?" I didn't want to hear the answer.

"The car is packed, and Daddy wants to get an early start," she said. "I know it's hard and I don't want to go, but we have to. I'll write to you every day, Lolo, I promise."

Tears were streaming down her cheeks as she turned and ran. I watched after her in shock and disbelief, and then I took off after her, not aware of the rocks digging into my bare feet. I created a big scene at the car, and Mr. Boxer finally just told the girls to get in the car. He said good-bye and drove away. Sandy was waving out the back window until we lost sight of each other.

After school got out for the summer, I stayed inside the house with shades drawn for the next two months. I pretty much stayed in my room. I finally decided to get out of the house and ride my bike to a movie to help myself feel better. It helped until I had to go back home. Then, I would end up in my room, alone again, and feeling sorry for myself.

Helen Trent on the radio just made me feel worse until I eventually turned a corner and just felt angry. That felt much better. It may be my best emotion.

I went to the five-and-dime and did a little shoplifting. That usually worked as a pick me up. Nothing big, just some lipstick and nail polish. I always paid for my movie magazines and True Romance.

It was almost Labor Day and school would be starting the following week. I needed a new uniform and shoes, so I walked down to my father's office. I wanted Margaret to take me shopping and I figured she would enjoy getting out of the office and spending more of my father's money. I missed her and we hadn't seen each other since Sandy left.

"Hey, Margaret," I said when I saw her sitting at her desk.

"Hey, Lolo," she answered without much enthusiasm.

It occurred to me that we both seemed sort of sad and bedraggled.

"I need some clothes for school, so can you take me shopping?"

She got up from her desk and said, "I'll ask your father."

She went into his office and I could see there was a lot of conversation going on. They seemed deep in negotiations, and then he gave her money and he went right back to his paperwork. It pissed me off that he couldn't even manage to give me a wave or a glance. Maybe he was too guilty to look me in the eye. Anyway, it would probably piss me off if he did or he didn't. I'm just pissed off these days.

As she walked out of his office towards me, I couldn't help noticing that she had put on a lot of weight. Her waist was as big as her butt. Or maybe it was the full skirt she was wearing instead of her usual tight skirt.

"Hey, you've gained weight," I said, stating the obvious.

She burst into tears.

"Jesus, Margaret, you're not that fat. Don't cry." I tried to apologize. Who knew she'd be so sensitive? Well, I guess that's a lesson. Never, ever, tell a woman her butt looks big.

She just wasn't any fun that day. I guess I wasn't fun either. Maybe we were a good pair? I couldn't wait to get the shopping over with and she seemed to feel the same way, but she managed to power through it and include a few super big tops for herself. Again, I didn't say anything. What the hell, take the old man for whatever you can get.

I thought we'd at least stop for something to eat, but no such luck. She dropped me off at my house. I invited her in, but she said she needed to get back to work which I knew was bullshit. I suspect she went to lunch without me and snagged another carton of cigs.

I didn't go back to my father's office until October hoping maybe Margaret would have forgotten our last tiff, and we could go shopping for some Halloween candy and a cool costume for me and whatever she was in the mood for. Sitting at her desk was a man.

"Who are you?" I asked.

"You must be Loretta. I'm Jeff."

"Where is Margaret?"

"Who?" he said and then added, "Oh, you must mean the lady who used to work here."

I walked straight into my father's office – something I had never done before. Anger trumps fear and good judgment. "Where is Margaret?" I demanded.

He looked up in surprise, and then an angry sneer crossed his face. "She quit. What do you want?"

I came right back at him. "I want to know what you did to her, and why you make everyone I care about to disappear?"

"How should I know? Probably, because you are such a brat. Now, what do you want? I'm busy."

"I want you to go to hell, Old Man."

Outside, in the cold air, my body was on fire. My jaw was clenched so tight that my teeth hurt. I just kept repeating to myself, *I hate you! I hate you!* I was so angry that I actually saw black for a few seconds. Like maybe I would pass out from hate. It was the same feeling I had in the car looking back at Miss Sarah disappearing that last day. "I hate you and I hope you die, Old Man."

I was certain my father had something to do with Margaret's disappearance. I didn't want to accept that maybe he was right; that it was all my fault for all of them leaving – my mother, Miss Sarah, Sandy, and now Margaret. Maybe it was even my fault that Mrs. Boxer died. If I wasn't so much trouble and didn't eat so much like a pig, then maybe I could have gone on vacation with them, and I could have stopped her from going swimming.

Sooner or later I would have to face the facts that nobody was ever going to be there for me. It was dangerous to be there for me. Nobody would ever love me. I hate me. Maybe even God hates me. I vowed I would never love anyone again, and I hoped that would keep me and us all safe.

School went on endlessly. The only joy was picking out the weakest and most willing classmates to follow my orders. We went on a rampage of smoking in the grotto, soaping windows, smashing pumpkins, stealing wine from Father Brockmeyer's stash, and setting off cherry bombs in people's trash cans.

Thanksgiving and Christmas came and went and nobody invited me over. I spent endless hours in my room writing how much I hated my father in my diary. I spent a lot of time at the movies during the holidays. The old man finally broke down and bought a television, but I mostly listened to music on the radio. I stayed in my room when I knew he was home. I now communicated with him only through Jeff, and then only when absolutely necessary.

13

Never Trust a Redhead

One day, I went to the office to talk to Jeff about getting me some money for a field trip that I made up to procure some serious cash for essentials. I am stashing money so at some point I can leave this hell hole.

I wish I had never gone to the office now. When I walked in, I saw that familiar red hair. I didn't need to see her face. I knew exactly who it was. Oh, thank God, my Margaret is back. I went barging into the office calling her name. At that point, an unrecognizable sound came from her as she stood up and turned around. She was holding a screaming baby.

"Whose baby is that?" I demanded, not really wanting to hear the answer unless it was "I found it outside."

"It's my baby. Do you want to hold her?"

"No! I don't like babies." I felt betrayed by this woman now. How dare she have a baby and not tell me? How dare she leave me for this little brat? I could hardly hear her over the noise this kid was making.

I got out of there so fast I forgot to tell Jeff to get money. For days, I couldn't stop thinking about the whole stupid mess. Never trust a redhead or a friend.

I had gotten one letter from Sandy. On the back of the envelope, it said. S.W.A.K. She explained that means "sealed with a kiss." She said she was having fun with her aunt and cousins. She and Patty were taking baton lessons and were cheerleaders at their new school. She had a boyfriend and the school had dances in the gym. Blah, blah, blah.

I wrote back and said "I have a boyfriend too, and he likes to take me to movies and kiss a lot. I have lots of friends at school this year, and I am having so much fun going to parties. My father got me a dog for Christmas, and I named him Jerry to go along with my new cat named Tom."

The letter was short, and I finished with "This will probably be my last letter for a long time because I am just too busy to write." Love Loretta. The Loretta part was on purpose. Sandy was no longer special enough to call me Lolo. I hope that hurt. I didn't write on the back of the envelope S.W.A.K. I hope she got the insult.

Valentine's Day is not the fun day it was in the lower grades when we exchanged cards, and you knew by the card who really liked you and who could give a shit. Now the only things to look forward to are heart-shaped cookies at lunch.

Sister told us a story about St. Valentine. He was a priest who married Christian couples so that the husbands wouldn't have to go to war. This upset the Emperor who was short of troops. When Saint Valentine refused to deny his faith in Jesus, he was beaten with clubs and stoned, but when that didn't kill him, they cut off his head. One of his miracles was that he restored the sight of his jailer's daughter and on the eve of his death, he sent her a note and signed it "Your Valentine." He is the patron Saint of happy marriages and young people. He did a bunch of other miracles after he died.

Anyway, the miracles of Saints are interesting, if you believe it, but the violence and suffering are the best part of the story for me, and that is the true lesson of life according to Sister

Mary Benedict, our religion teacher. Offer it up and you will get your reward in Heaven. No thanks, Sister, I'll cash my check here.

It is the first of March. Will the sun ever come out? Will it ever stop snowing?

The buzz around the school is all about Sister Mary John getting sick and puking all over her desk. She ran out of the room. Several of the students went up to get a better look and made gagging noises on the way back to their seats. When Sister came back and cleaned it up, she told the class not to tell anyone.

"Yes, Sister. Of course, Sister." That's hilarious! The word spread like wildfire.

The big news is that I'm finally getting boobs! At first, I thought I was getting cancer because they hurt and were like hard marbles. I thought maybe I had a tumor, but now they have stopped hurting. I hope they get a lot bigger.

14

Sex, Drugs and Rock n' Roll

I have made three new friends: Ginny, Donna, and Bonnie. They don't go to Blessed Sacrament. They go to public school.

I met them at the Dew Drop Inn on Saturday. Ginny came up to me while I was finishing my French fries and cherry Coke. I was lighting a cigarette and she asked if she could bum one. I said sure and she sat down in my booth.

We started chatting, mostly about music. She asked me if I knew about Elvis Presley. I did not. She said she moved here from Memphis, Tennessee, and he was from there. She had seen him in person, and he was going to be on the *Hayride* that night and did I want to come to her house to see him. Hell yes! I'm so glad that I did because it changed my life. I mean, I will never be the same.

More about Elvis later, but first I'll tell you about Ginny. Her real name is Virginia and she is 13, almost 14, and in high school. She is already a teenager. Ginny is pretty, but her teeth are all rotten, green and black. When she laughs, she keeps her upper lip pulled over her teeth and covers her mouth with her hand.

She is funny and makes me laugh. I love to hear her talk because she has a southern drawl that I am trying to mimic. She says things like "I'm fixin' to go to town." She has dishwater blonde hair and green eyes. She wears tight Levi's and wears her collar turned up on her shirt. She looks tough, like a hood, and I want to dress just like her. She has opened my eyes to a whole new world of music and teenage delinquency.

That first night when I went to her house, I was shocked. Ginny's mom and dad were drinking beer and cursing at each other, but they also laughed a lot and seemed to be enjoying themselves despite being surrounded by their squalor. The family is dirt poor with about 12 kids. I don't think her mother even knows how many kids she has.

Whenever I have seen Ginny's mom, she always looks tired and her hair always needs washing and combing. Their house is a total dump. It's not just cluttered, but dirty chaos. Clothes go from the clothesline to a basket where people search for something to wear. Everything is wrinkled and gray. The boys in the family are ornery and dirty in every way. I never want to go there, and if I must, I don't want to stay very long because of all this, plus it is a long, long walk from my house. They live at the edge of town by the railroad tracks. So, Ginny and I usually meet downtown after school and on weekends.

She has introduced me to her two friends, Donna and Bonnie. We like to stand around on the corner of Main Street, snapping our gum and smoking cigarettes and acting like we weren't waiting for boys to drive by and notice us. They yell out the window at us "Hey baby, I got something big just for you." We think, "Oh man, we must be so cool for a guy to say that."

We are having so much fun that I'm planning on going to public school next year so I can be with my new gang. I've had enough Catholics. I don't need any religion for that matter. It's all a big scam to keep the poor from killing the rich. I'm never going to church again.

On Saturday night, the JCs put on a dance, and it is broadcast on the radio by the local DJ. It is called JC's Saturday night. You have to be at least 13 to attend and it is definitely "the" place to be. I have devotedly tuned in at 9:00 p.m. every Saturday night for the last two years and danced in my room and dreamed of being there.

Finally, Ginny and Donna convince me that I can pass for 13 and no one will card me, so I should come with them. I bought a padded bra to accompany my "cool" Levi's that zipped up the front, not the side. I turn my collar up and put on my new white penny loafers. I wear lots of lipstick and mascara. Donna says I look like a cheap hooker. I know! I look great!

Sweet Jesus, it is better than I had even imagined! Boys and rock 'n roll! I just stand around and watch, hoping no one will ask me to dance because I don't know how.

I find my idol right away. Her name I learned is Vicki Pratt. She is petite but with a really neat figure. She has her brown hair cut in a "DA" in the back like Elvis. She wears a tight straight skirt, white tennis shoes and bobby socks. The ultimate in cool is the black pocket comb she sticks in the side of her sock by her ankle. I immediately buy a black pocket comb and emulate my heroine. She is the best dancer, and everyone pretty much surrounds her and watches her do a dance I've never witnessed before and will never see on Bandstand. It is called "the dirty boogie."

Ginny figures it out pretty quick and tries to teach the rest of us how to do it. I never can pull it off, but we make her repeat it endlessly until she tells us to forget it. Will I ever be so cool? The answer was no, never. I lack rhythm and confidence. I try to fix my hair in a "DA" but finally settled for a Natalie Wood's pixie. The hair struggle takes hours, but it is perhaps the most important detail. If your hair looks like shit, no amount of makeup or cool outfits can compensate. Might as well put on a stained shirt and stay home.

Donna is a big girl. She stands 5'10" and has a fully developed double D cup. She is oversexed with raging hormones. She is only 14 but she can actually pass for 18 and is in charge of buying us beer. I am in charge of paying for the beer and cigarettes.

Once, while standing on the corner, some boys yelled stuff and she yelled something back and they called her "Baby Huey," but she didn't hear it right so Ginny said, "they called you baby, honey." I thought that was kind of her and a lesson in charity for us all.

One Saturday night at JC's, we stepped out for a smoke when a car full of boys drove up to us and stopped to chat. After talking for a while, Donna got in the car with them and rode off. When she didn't come back after half an hour, we got scared because her mother would be picking us up at 10 and if she wasn't back what the hell would we say?

She did show up at the eleventh hour and enthusiastically gave us detailed information regarding the male penis. She was an attentive student apparently, and an equally good relater of technical information. She described each part and how it functioned, how to handle it, and what to expect if you handled it too long. While this was interesting, to say the least, I could have taught that class in fourth grade, but I acted like it was all news to me.

Donna's mother, father, and older brother were also giants. Her mother was very funny and open about sexual matters, which I really appreciated. She had those double D's and then some and would tell jokes like, "One time I got so depressed I decided to end it all. I called my Doctor and asked him where my heart was so I could shoot myself. He said it was just under my left breast so I shot myself in the kneecap."

Then she would sing, "Do your boobs hang low? Do they wobble two and fro? Can you tie them in a knot? Can you tie them in a bow?" That, of course, was hilarious to a 12-year-old.

Or she would say "What should we do? Go to the Y and swim or go to the A and P?" She also taught us a secret language. It was a year of only speaking pig Latin after that. "Oda ouya antway ota oga ota oolscha?" "Ona!"

Donna's mom would take us all to the Drive-in movie on "buck night" and would let us go sit in the chairs outside of the concession stand, where the dateless boys would come to pick up girls in hopes of getting to second base. She was a good sport and didn't come to check up on us even though she probably knew what was going on. We always took a blanket with us . . . in case we got cold. Yeah, right.

Every day during summer vacation, we hitched to the lake beach house where we rarely swam, except to wade and cool off. We certainly didn't want to get our hair wet. It was mostly about getting a tan using baby oil, being seen in our new suits, and dancing in the pavilion to the jukebox. The other reason I couldn't get wet above the waist was that I had stuffed my bathing suit with my padded bra to look like I had boobs. When will these things ever grow?

That summer before going into the 8th grade was the best summer I can remember – with the exception of being at Miss Sarah's, but those days were long gone.

I didn't get to go to public school in September like I had planned. So, I had to deal with one more year of nuns. I swear they had it in for us eighth graders since it was the last year they got to torture us. If they could have used the 'rack,' they probably would have.

But who cared? Not me with my posse and Elvis to focus on.

I believed that as an 8th grader, I would be looked up to and hopefully emulated by my lowly fan club of 5th, 6th and 7th graders who would instinctively know their place. Part of the status of being an 8th grader, and so everyone would know you were top dog, was that I would get to wear those long ribbons that I so coveted when Sandy and Patty wore them.

After seeing Elvis on TV, I was in love. I had never seen anything so wonderful, exciting and sexy in my life. Thus, began my love affair with Elvis. I collected every magazine that had his picture in it. I cut the pictures out and began to wallpaper my room. By the end of the year, every square inch of my room was covered with his lips, his pompadour, his hips, and sideburns. Girls would come to ogle, adore, kiss, and worship my shrine to the King. This creation of mine was my Queendom, and my claim to fame that year.

Finally, after I turned 13, for my birthday present, I got my first period. Thank you, Jesus!

Whoops, be careful what you wish for. This was not all it was cracked up to be. In fact, I lay in bed for two days with terrible cramps. Is this what I have to look forward to every month for the rest of my life? I didn't even have any Kotex on hand, except for the sample one Sandy left with me. Fortunately, the flow was very light, and I had time after I could get up and walk again, to get to the store.

My first experience of buying Kotex was humiliating. The stupid cashier asked if I needed a bag. "No asshole, I'll wear them home." I didn't actually say that, but what a jerk. Well, he was just a boy. Still, that's no excuse. By the way, I now know what it means when girls say, "Aunt Flo has come to visit."

Along with the cramps, my face breaks out in zits the size of Mount Vesuvius. What the fuck! Sorry, I just read *Catcher In*

The Rye and I can't stop saying fuck and goddamn it. It even got me sent to Sister's office once. There's always a Judas in the crowd ready to sell you out. I had no excuse because that book was on the "do not read list," which of course made everyone read it.

15
Lucky Lucy

Summer and graduation were practically here. I could smell the baby oil already. The very, very important – no, the most important quest now – was for the perfect bathing suit. We all decided to meet downtown on Saturday and begin the search.

Ginny didn't have any money as usual and Donna was pretty short on cash too, so we decided we would shoplift. It would be easy. We would just take several suits into the dressing room and wear one out under our clothes. Bonnie said she didn't want to do it so she stayed home. Chicken!

Saturday, we met downtown and made our plan. We decided not to go into the dressing room together. Two will go in and one would stay out and go back and forth with suits. We will dazzle them with our footwork. Every now and then, we will complain about how nothing looks good. When all three of us have our suits on under our baggy sweatshirts, we will make a big deal of asking when the next shipment will be coming in to pick from because we just didn't find anything we liked this time.

We left the store and walked about a block thinking we had pulled off the great bank robbery when a policeman came up to us and said we were under arrest. Off we go to the police station where we are stripped down to the suits. We were taken individually to our respective homes or, in my case, the dreaded office. To say the least, my father was not happy, especially when he found out he had to take off work to go to juvenile court.

I was placed on probation and confined to my house for the summer. The other girls just got probation and had to report once a month, but my father's punishment was also house confinement. I had limited access to the outside world other than finishing the 8th grade, but excluding any celebration of the graduation.

"You know who" employed a woman to come to the house every day to keep an eye on me. Her name was Lucille, but I referred to her as Lucky Lucy. It could have been Lazy Lucy because she never left the couch, but she was lucky because she ate all our food and didn't have to do shit for her $.50 an hour. She was glued to daytime soaps and responded like these characters were her best friends.

I made the best of my incarceration by working on my tan and reading. Mostly I read romance and movie magazines, but also an occasional book from our bookshelves. They must have been my mother's because as far as I know "you know who" has never read a book.

Twice a week, Donna would make the trip over to my house with cigarettes and new magazines that I paid for, which also included her cigarettes and an extra buck for her trouble. On her next visit, she gets my old magazines, so she thinks this is a "saaweet deal." She considers this her summer job.

Lucy didn't care if Donna hung around, so that was a gold star for Lucy. Donna and I would get all greased up, put the radio on the back steps tuned into our favorite rock n' roll station out of Chicago, and bake in the sun, drinking Coke until we were sufficiently cooked. Once in a while, we would watch one of Lucy's soaps or engage her in a game of rummy.

I told Donna not to come on Wednesdays because I loved spending time with Miss Sarah. I helped her clean house and cook just to be around her. She and I had long talks over frying chicken. I told her I was going to Rockton High in September and I was through with nuns. She said, "Whatever, Lolo. It is time to make new friends and get a fresh start." She advised me to dump Donna and find some nice girls to do stuff with. That proved to be good advice which unfortunately I did not take.

Rockton High was a whole different world from Blessed Sacrament, and not just because it was high school. Boys and girls could make out in plain sight. Kids would sit in the halls, legs stretched out, books scattered everywhere, and teachers would have to navigate over them. No one said "Good Morning" to any of the teachers or treated them with any respect like I was accustomed to, but I fell in with this new system effortlessly. We are all reduced to the lowest denominator.

It was fine to be a freshman because I had sophomore friends and that made me feel like I was cool, even with a face full of pimples. So why was I popular with Donna and Ginny? Simple. I had the cash. I could buy cigarettes and beer and pretty much anything else we needed. The good thing about having a drunk for a father was that he left money lying around and didn't know or care if any of it was going missing.

Now it was the three of us. Me, Donna and Ginny. Bonnie had found new friends after the bathing suit scandal. We were the bad girls, and nobody messed with us. But nobody messed with us in a good way either.

You can tell who people are by their clothes. The Sandra Dee types wear nylons and flats with skirts and sweater sets. They are the cheerleaders who get pregnant in senior year or right out of high school. This is their time to shine.

The academics have no sense of style. Their mothers probably pick out their clothes. They don't have dates and will go to college and have short careers before marrying their college sweethearts. Then, they'll volunteer for the PTA.

We had our uniform of white tennis shoes, shirts with the collar up and Lucky Strikes rolled up in the sleeve, and tight Levi's. Don't forget the comb in one sock. I have no illusions about where we'll end up.

I had to take the bus to school now. I rode downtown and then transferred to the bus that took me to Rockton High. The three of us met downtown and transferred together. We smoked one cigarette after another all the way to school. When the bus doors opened, we descended in a cloud of smoke.

After school, we hung out at the Dew Drop Inn or Walgreen's, stuffing nickels into the jukebox and consuming large quantities of Cherry Cokes, fries, and more cigarettes. I was up to two packs a day. My index finger and middle finger sports a yellow nicotine stain that won't wash off. I'm beginning to wheeze with the slightest exercise.

Conversations consist of trash talking about teachers, students, parents and anyone within our line of vision. Sometimes we just razz each other out of boredom.

"I've decided to let my hair grow out. No matter how many pictures I take to the beauty shop these plow jockeys just can't get it right. So, I'm just gonna let it grow."

"Yeah, let it grow over your face. That will be an improvement."

"Hey, I'm not as dumb as I look."

"How could you be?"

"Thanks, Donna. We're a good match. Your face and my ass."

There's usually some truth to any joking. I am tired of paying five dollars for a good pixie cut and all I get is a good cry. I do have good hair. It's thick and has a natural wave. Maybe it just isn't right for a pixie and maybe I can hide some of my zits with it longer. I need to find my look and I need a thing . . . a thing that is just mine, besides my Elvis room.

It takes me almost the whole year to find my talent, but I finally get it. I can shimmy. I can shimmy all the way back until my head almost meets the ground, and then shimmy back up again.

The first time I demonstrate this amazing talent at the Dew Drop, it was quite a crowd pleaser. Donna wants to learn how and so does Ginny and a few onlookers, too. Donna cannot get it right. Those double D's are her Achilles' heels. Ginny gets it but cannot bend back very far. Hard as she may try, she can't quite do it. It's all my thing and only mine.

Finally, June arrives and we are free for the summer. Our shenanigans during the year show up in our final grades. I get straight D's. Considering the lack of effort we put in, and the times we cut class or failed to show up at all, those are more than fair grades. I suspect it was to just keep us moving on. Anyway, I'm the high achiever in my gang of three.

My probation officer will be proud. He enjoys being right. He tells me my rebellious attitude is not going to serve me in the future, but he doesn't know the half of it. Smoking, drinking, skipping school and still pushing the limits with some petty thefts makes me feel in control. It does serve me. It's a coping skill and that's all I can think of to do.

Summer is filled with beach time, working on a tan, dancing in the pavilion, and hangin' on the corner of 5th and Main. None of us has a boyfriend, and dates consist of hand jobs in the back seat of cars at the roller rink. I'm giving hand jobs. I don't know what Donna and Ginny are giving.

We also constantly have them page our "friend" Mike Hunt over the PA system. "Mike Hunt, Mike Hunt, please come to the front desk. Is Mike Hunt here?" This is hilarious to us, and many of the boys get it too. Sure, it's all fun and games until someone gets a black eye. Ginny got into a fight with a girl who called her a skank. That, plus Mike Hunt, got us thrown out permanently. We are "persona non grata" now.

16

Mercury Blues

By August, we are bored out of our minds. Donna's mom had a heart attack or something and landed in the hospital for a week. When she came home, she was not her old self and just laid around on the couch. We had to hitch to the beach or walk everywhere. She didn't want to go to the drive-in movies, and she said she couldn't drive us to the JC Saturday Night dance club either.

There are only a couple of summer vacation weeks left, and Donna and Ginny are at my house working on a plan. We need to get to the JC dance, but how?

"Why don't we take my dad's Mercury?" I suggest. "It's just sitting in the garage because he took the truck this morning."

"Do you have the keys?" Ginny asked.

"I think he usually leaves them under the floor mat. Let's go see."

"Hey, we can be back before he gets home. He stays out really late on Saturday nights, right?"

"Well, yeah, but it's a stick shift. Who knows how to drive a stick shift?"

"I know how," Donna volunteers.

"Okay. What are we waiting for?"

And just that easy, we stole a car. Gears–a-grinding, we got downtown and never took it out of second gear. Donna was only slightly familiar with a stick shift. I guess we had fun. I remember doing my "thing" to an adoring crowd. Well, that's how I remember it, but most of the night I was just nervous and jerky and wanted it to end. Common sense kicked in a little too late.

We took Ginny home and Donna said she would just stay overnight at my house and walk home in the morning. We got about a mile from Ginny's and shit, shit, shit. Red lights flashing in the rearview mirror. We couldn't even attempt to outrun them in second gear. We pulled over and got handcuffed and taken off to jail.

Grand Theft Auto is a felony and prison is possible, or so my probation officer tells me. Donna and I didn't have time to concoct a feasible lie like she was taking me to the emergency room or something. Nope, we were separated, and like a rat abandoning a sinking ship, I blamed it all on her. What a pal, what a buddy. What are friends for?

I spent the night in jail and realize it is a place I do not wish to see again. My father never liked Donna and this was a nice way of getting rid of her, and me. Long story short, due to my father's influence with the Chief of Police and the Rockton justice system, Donna was sent to reform school and I was sent to a Catholic boarding school several states away.

17

Going to Hell

The train ride to Sacred Heart Academy was a new experience, but not that exciting. I watched the flat cornfields fly by, one after another. Occasionally there would be a small town. Shacks along the tracks reminded me of Ginny. Usually, some dirty little ragamuffins would run alongside the train waving and sometimes throwing rocks. I usually waved back or gave them the finger. Lucy slept most of the time, except when we went to the dining car to eat. That was the best part of the trip. Lucky Lucy is still getting paid to sleep and eat and now gets to see the world or at least some part of the world other than Rockton. Nice job.

Ten hours and one transfer later we were there. The town didn't look too much different from Rockton. Maybe it was a little bigger, but I didn't get to see that much of it on the taxi ride to the school.

Lucy asked the taxi driver to wait. She said she wouldn't be very long. The school looked beautiful from the outside. Green grass, nicely manicured grounds and a big statue of the Blessed Mother out front.

I took a deep breath as Lucy and I walked into the building. Just a few feet from the entrance I saw a sign over an open door: Sister Mary Joseph Principal. As soon as Sister came out,

Lucy gave her an envelope and said her good-byes. Lucky Lucy gave her usual minimal effort.

Sister looks like an angry cherub, but then she smiles, and I feel like she might be one of the good ones. I do love my nuns, like Sister Theresa who should be canonized. But then, there are the few who I think will go straight to hell. I do appreciate them more now that I have spent time at Rockton High. Of all the orders I think the Dominican's are the best. I love the outfits! I mean habits.

Sister invites me in to have a seat in her office. She scrutinizes the contents of the envelope for what seems an eternity. I am praying it doesn't say anything about my probation or incarceration or that I am a horrible skank. When she finishes, she looks at me with a critical eye. I swallow hard to keep from throwing up. Eventually, she speaks. "What do you expect to learn here, Loretta?"

I wonder if this is a trick question, and my mind is spinning, looking for a suitable answer.

"I hope to learn how to be worthy in the eyes of God and get a good education." I blink or twitch, not sure which is actually happening, but I amazed myself and wonder where did I pull that out of? Then I remembered to say "Sister." There was probably too long of a pause before I said Sister, or maybe Sister Joseph is that easy to bullshit. She did not acknowledge what I thought was a brilliant answer. Instead, she asked what activities were of interest to me?

Yikes, was I auditioning for Miss America? "Well, Sister, I enjoy cooking and baking and music. I also enjoy reading, especially about the Saints." Good save with that one. I smile sweetly.

"Very well, Loretta. Who is your favorite Saint?"

"Oh, Sister, there are so many it's hard to just choose one." I hope that takes care of that. Again, I think, well done Loretta. But I celebrate too soon.

"Well, why don't you just give me one that comes to mind."

"Ah, um, ok, well, I really like St. Valentine."

"And why is that, Loretta?"

"I guess because he is the patron saint of happy marriages and love. And isn't love the most important thing in the world? I mean, Jesus said to love one another."

Jesus H. Christ, please let this be over. Apparently, my prayer was answered for now, and Sister went on to what "you know who" has requested in his letter.

"Your father has asked that you pay for part of your tuition by working in the school. I believe we have just found a good match for your talents. You will be assigned to the kitchen with Sister Diane to further your interest in cooking."

"Oh. That sounds like fun, Sister." That cheap bastard must stay up nights thinking of new ways to make me miserable. I hope he chokes on his next meal. I am starting to itch because I really need a cigarette. I have some stashed in my suitcase and I am trying to think of where and how I can at least get a couple of drags.

What I didn't know then was that I would be rooming with a senior, who would be the good influence that was supposed to rub off on me. A rollaway bed was put in with my first roommate, Saint Martina.

I want to make her my best new friend like Miss Sarah suggested, so I open my whole life to her during our first hours together. I realize I am talking too much and too fast, but I really need a nicotine fix.

18
Saint Martina

Martina is so perfect she is boring. I feel judged all the time, so no wonder at the first opportunity I snoop through her stuff and read her private story. It is surprising, and boring – except for the bloody parts. She writes:

I am writing as a process to understand who I am and to express my feelings about my life. I have no one. My parents were killed in a highway accident when I was seven years old. I was old enough to still have cogent memories of them but too young to comprehend the magnitude of the tragedy of it all.

The continuing tragedy is that I was "taken in" by my aunt and uncle. My dad's brother and his wife had no children of their own. I think they don't particularly like children. Before my parents died, whenever we would visit them, I was to be seen, but not heard. I think they really didn't know what else to do. Aunt Marcella (I call her Auntie M, but only in secret), both she and Uncle Mark (Uncle M) treated me like I was some creature from outer space who resembled a miniature human.

What a shock when I ended up living with them. Uncle M owns a hardware store and they live in a luxurious ranch style home with a big picture window and an attached garage. All this opulence is not where I came from. The guest room is my bedroom at the far end of the home so I will not interrupt their social life at all, and they still have plenty of room for visiting relatives that I do not know, and they do not care to know me.

The carpeting is so plush in my room that my feet almost disappear when I walk on it. Next, to my room, I have my own bathroom all to myself. Auntie M and Uncle M have their own connected to their bedroom. I only saw it once when I first arrived and was given the tour of the whole place so I would be oriented to my surroundings and know what was off limits.

So, all in all, we could pretty much cohabitate without inter-fering with each other and I liked that, knowing the way they felt about children. I could stay out of their sight and out of mind.

We all ate breakfast together before Uncle M left for the store and I eventually trotted to school. I think this made them lose their fear of me and I of them. We eventually became reluctant friends. The best part, of course, is that I knew I was not a financial burden to them, and I liked their house much better than the two-bedroom bungalow I had grown up in with my parents.

It is annoying that I have to read Martina's story a little at a time when she isn't around. At this point, all I can say is "*Boo hoo*, you have to live with rich people who leave you alone. I mean, big deal. Try living with a drunk who hates you every stinking day of your life." Well, I guess we have the dead mother thing in common, and that makes me feel bad for her, but who says things like 'cogent' and 'cohabitate' and 'opu-lence'? Nobody talks like that in real life and what's a bunga-low? I have to go look this stuff up. What a pain!

The next time I get my hands on her story, she has hidden it under her mattress. She'll have to do better than that. Clearly, she doesn't know who she is dealing with, although she did know she needed to hide it.

Her story continues:

I didn't make many friends at school because I decided that since I was more or less alone in the world, I should take a scholastic route rather than a social one. I rather liked learning and became very proficient at the traditional three "Rs" and much to my surprise, I was described as a "brain."

I knew I couldn't expect Uncle M to support me forever. They had enough money for sure, but they were not generous, especially with me. They provided me only with the things I needed, and I understood there was no question about getting the things I wanted.

The years went by and finally, I was in the 8th grade. I looked forward to the graduation in June. However, elation turned to fear when I got my first period. At the time, I didn't know what was happening. I saw that I was bleeding when I peed, and my stomach began to hurt badly. In a panic, I took some aspirin and started putting cold packs on my stomach. That helped the cramps.

So far, I hadn't stained the bed, which I was terrified of doing because Auntie M had a silk fetish – probably because she read too many Pearl S. Buck books about China. She had silk all over the place – drapes, bedding, and silk underwear. Uncle M had silk suits, ties and of course silk stockings. Everything had to be dry cleaned, especially the shantung type. Auntie M would not appreciate blood-stained sheets.

Since I had no one to confide in, I decided to consult the school nurse, who of course told me all about menstruation and gifted me with a large box of Kotex and told me how to use them. I was so happy that I had gone to her and even happier that I wasn't dying from a tumor or something!

I decided I would try to make friends with other girls because the nurse said it happened to most females around 14. I figured there would be strength in numbers. The problem was how to do it. Once again, I had no one to turn to or confide in, and I kind of kicked myself for not being more sociable to begin with. It was only weeks before summer vacation.

I had to stop reading again just when it was maybe getting good. I see that we both had practically the same experience with "Aunt Flo." I wonder if this is a common thing.

I am now hooked on Martina's use of big words and I am getting "proficient" using the dictionary in the study hall and that makes me feel "elated." I have subsequently come up with a few words of my own.

If I was on a desert island and only had one book to take, I know it would be a dictionary. Certainly, not the Bible, but what do I know? I never read the Bible. Catholics don't even want you to read the Bible. Leave that to the professionals. They will tell you what to think.

The next time I read her story, I feel a little sorry for her, but then again, what a baby! Waaaa!

Her story continues:

Then my opportunity came when I went to the public library and there was a notice about a summer reading book club for teens 13 to 17. It would meet once a week at the library conference room and there would be a different recommended book of the week to be discussed that following week. The first book was Charlotte's Web. I immediately went to see if I could check it out but feared there might not be a copy left. The librarian said she would look, but mostly you were expected to have your own copy. I couldn't imagine how much anyone could find to write about spiders, but I had set myself on this path of being a joiner and not a loner, and I needed to succeed. The grief of so quickly losing my parents has somewhat subsided, but I still want to live a life they would be proud of, just in case they are watching me from somewhere. The librarian returned and said there was a copy left so I was in luck, and I believed it was because they were watching over me.

I hoped my allowance would cover buying any future books that I couldn't get at the library so I checked with a couple of bookstores on prices of books and was relieved to discover I would probably be fine.

I can't help thinking she needs to learn the five-finger discount method, but then again, she's Saint Martina so it's hopeless. I can't wait to sneak a peek at the rest of the story. I'm on pins and needles. I am being slightly facetious. Take that Martina. What's next . . .

Monday night book club arrived and I was really nervous when I saw about 20 teens, some I recognized from my grade school. Mrs. Campion facilitated and we all sat in a circle and were required to say our names, ages, and a little about ourselves, mostly why we were there.

When it was my turn, I could feel my cheeks getting hot and they all turned their attention to me. I wished I had some public speaking experience before this. I was so choked up that I thought I might not be able to say anything, but I said, "I am Martina Blankenship and I live on Coyote Drive. I am 14 and hope that this club will improve my reading and comprehension skills, as well as social ones." Everyone clapped politely, as they did for all the others, but it made me feel more confident anyway. I think I did all right.

When introductions were over, Mrs. Campion proceeded with a question and answer session and I found it really challenging to respond in an articulate way. A few others seemed to express themselves easily. I didn't contribute very much, but I am a good listener and a quick learner. Next time

I will do better. The evening went very fast and I was sorry when it was over. It was the most interesting evening of my life thus far.

Auntie M picked me up of course, but while I was waiting for her, one of the boys in the club asked if I needed a ride home. His name was Chris and I had noticed him during the session because he was so handsome, and also very smart. He had his own car and sadly he didn't pick me out of the crowd. He asked a group of kids who all piled into his red convertible. I wished I didn't have a ride and could be one of his group. I could hardly wait for the next book club meeting.

Then I got my period again and found that my allowance wouldn't cover both sanitary pads and the book of the week which was Oliver Twist *by Charles Dickens. It was a book I keenly identified with as he was an orphan too, through no choice of his own.*

Uncle M left for the store right after breakfast so I took the opportunity to talk to Auntie M in private. I jumped right into it.

"Aunt Marcella, I started having periods last month and the school nurse gave me enough pads to make it through that and the next time but with having to buy my own books for the book club and pads also, I don't think my allowance will cover both. Could you help out?"

Auntie M looked at me with a face I had not seen before. Her brown eyes turned black and she gasped, "You started having periods and didn't tell me? Why?"

"Oh, I didn't want to bother you and besides isn't that the kind of thing the school nurse is for?"

"I need to know something like that while you're under my care. It means you are capable of getting pregnant and having a baby, and I wouldn't want that to happen until you are safely

married or living on your own. Did the school nurse tell you that? And have you been going around with any boys without my knowing?"

"Oh no," I pleaded my innocence.

"How about that book club? Are there any boys there?"

"Just four or five and they mostly stick together. I think they are there for self-improvement like me. I don't even know all their names yet."

Auntie M gave a big sigh and said (mostly to herself), "I was afraid of something like this."

I was taken aback by her reaction or over-reaction to my news, but I guess that is why I didn't tell her in the first place. I have finally realized what a burden I am to them. The demon has emerged, and it is a bloody one.

She then took on the additional irritation of negotiating my new allowance. She agreed to subsidize my debts until I can find a part-time job and pay her back in the fall when I turn 15. Unexpectedly, she patted my hand and said, "That's a good girl." She dug around in her purse and came up with a $5 bill which I took gratefully and said so.

"I also want to save money because I want to go to a good college," I told her. "The part-time job won't interfere with my grades, I promise."

Little did I know I wouldn't need a part-time job because she had already made up her mind that I was a danger to myself, and she would not be responsible if I should get myself in the family way, so that is how I ended up in boarding school. In order to keep me away from male predators since I was now pubescent, M&M decided they didn't want me to be exposed to the vagaries of public high school. Instead, my virginity would be carefully watched and guarded by the holy nuns. We weren't even Catholic and the tuition, of course, was much higher, but

M&M didn't mind because it ensured their peace of mind.

There were pages I didn't have time to read so I skipped to the end, and her final entry made me go to a dictionary again to figure out what she was saying about me. I knew it wouldn't be good, but "ameliorate and meretricious?" Really, bitch?"

Good grief, it's hard to have sympathy for a girl as smart and pretty as Martina. How could a senior in high school be such an ignoramus about life and such a pushover? I'd help her but I have my own troubles, and by the way, she's one of them. I got caught smoking in the bathroom and she told Sister where my cigs were stashed. What a snitch and a bitch! So now along with my KP duties, I have to scrub some floors on my hands and knees no less. Thanks, Martina, and boohoo, and oh yeah, watch out!

19

There's a Lesson

This has been the longest three weeks of my life. It is literally "Holy Hell." I've been on my knees for most of it. Six o'clock Mass every morning. Breakfast usually consists of oatmeal or Cream of Wheat and toast, which is preferable to the dried out scrambled eggs. But we can always count on the ever-present stewed prunes. (Holy shit!)

By then it is seven-thirty, and I work in the kitchen until eight when the bell rings for class. I grab my books and dash for homeroom which is also Religion class which includes Latin. Then algebra, English, study hall and lunch.

By that time, I am starving, and everything is delicious. After lunch, I scrape the dirty dishes and also eat whatever desserts are left over or half eaten. I am sublimating (my new word of the day) food for nicotine. The bell rings and I am off to history class, art or music or phys-ed, science, and study hall. I try to get all my homework done in study hall. The bell rings and I envy the day students who get to leave school.

In the evening, after Vespers, there is leisure time if you have all your homework finished. The leisure room has carefully pre-selected TV programs (boring), Monopoly (what are we 10?) and bridge (Hello, Grandma). Once a week we could dance in the room where we have PE, which might have been fun if there had been any boys to dance with. Some girls prefer to just sit in their cliques and talk. I have no idea what they talk about. Don't you have to have a life to have something to say?

I use this time to take a shower when no one is around. I think I will be mocked because of my small breasts. I would be President of the "Itty Bitty Titty Committee" if there was one. The shower relaxes me, and also, that way I don't have to take a shower in the morning. I would rather sleep for an extra ten minutes.

Martina never joins any groups in the leisure room and neither do I. She prefers to listen to some disc jockey on the radio every night. He does have a nice voice and sometimes says something funny. His program goes on into the late evening. After lights are out and Sister does her bed checks, Martina turns the radio back on very low. I like it because it puts me to sleep.

One night in the dark I ask her what she likes about this particular program. Is it the music or the man? There is a long silence and I think she is not going to answer, but then she begins.

"It is the man and his mind. He is passionate about every subject he brings up. He is deep and sensitive even though he is young." She continues to talk about him as if she knows him intimately.

In the dark, I am mesmerized by her voice. It is serene. Sweet and smooth like Skippy peanut butter. Her voice is a little breathy and her diction is impeccable. Her innate ability to draw me in so I hang on her every word makes me want to keep her talking. I ask her more. "How do you know he is young? He could be like the Wizard of Oz, hiding behind the curtain."

"I know what he looks like. I saw him downtown at an opening of the record store last month. He is handsome and charismatic."

"Did you speak to him?"

"Oh no, there were lots of girls hanging around his booth. I wouldn't know what to say anyway."

"Martina, you have a face and a figure that send men walking into walls and you don't even know it. You don't have to take a back seat to anyone. If I had your looks and your smarts, the world would be my oyster. I would create a dream so big that everyone would fall all over themselves to be in my presence."

"Don't be silly, Loretta. I'm just being realistic. And by the way, you are pretty, and as soon as your acne clears up, you will be beautiful."

This is a huge moment. Even though I think she is bullshitting me, I realize that we are now friends or could be friends. I am determined to push her into discovering her power. Let the transformation begin! I fall asleep in the comfort that all is right with the night.

The next night I probe to see if she will reveal more to me. "Martina, I told you about my family and why I am here. Why are you here?" Of course, I haven't told her anything really personal about my life. My dirty little secret is safe.

She tells me the story of living with M&M and how Auntie M's fears put her here. Then she says she has never even kissed a boy and she doesn't believe she is pretty because no boys have ever paid any attention to her.

"Martina, boys are stupid. They were just intimidated by your looks. Besides, you are rather shy which could be interpreted as being stuck up. Anyway, you were just in elementary school, so you didn't have a true opportunity. And your Aunt M could see that boys would soon be flocking to your door. She isn't afraid of you getting pregnant and ruining your life. She is afraid you'll ruin her reputation. It's all about her, but what about you? Let go of your desire for M&M's acceptance, because the harder you try, the less likely you are to get it. What do you want? What is your dream?"

She ponders this question for a while. She thinks too much. She's all in her head. When she does open up, she says she wants to go to college and then teach. Really? That's the big dream for her life? Can she really be that vapid or have Auntie M and the nuns stripped her of any zest for life? Have they filled her with so much fear that becoming a teacher is all she is willing to risk?

Martina challenges me with her intellectual focus on life. She tries to convince me this is what she really wants, but where's the passion? It feels more like this is what other people want her to do or what she thinks is expected of her. I think I am her only friend ever. I can't let her down.

I take another avenue; one she may identify with. "Have you ever thought that it is your spiritual obligation to fulfill your potential for the glory of God? It isn't just men who have the right to take risks to search for the Holy Grail."

These conversations in the dark make it safe to say things you wouldn't say in the light of day, and I can tell that Martina is getting a glimpse of possibilities for her life that she has never before imagined.

The next night I brought it up again. "You lack confidence and a vision because that's a mother's job to give you those, and Auntie M had no mothering skills. Have you read any books about strong women? Not saints; that's not the kind of example I'm talking about."

She says she had read one book about Eleanor Roosevelt when she was in a book club. I tell her to read some more. We fall asleep thinking about it and listening to her sweet Jerry Fox on the radio.

20

Take My Advice; I'm Not Using It

I give Martina confidence and courage and she teaches me to accept and surrender the struggle to be in control. I know she is right, so I offer my suffering up. I perform my duties and commit to my studies to the best of my ability.

I have let go of the desire to debate Sister in religion class. Maybe it is all true. Nobody knows for sure. I do feel some internal stirring during Mass, and what can explain the dialogue that comes out of me in the dark with Martina? It feels like Spirit is speaking through me, or maybe I am just putting myself in her skin. It's what I would do if I had all her beauty and brains. Either way, we are giving each other what we need right now.

There is a day student who always sits next to me in study hall. We have only acknowledged one another without words until today. Sister leaves the room and my neighbor says, "Do you have the answer to the first equation today?"

I do, but only because my neighbor in algebra lets me copy her work. This request is a conundrum. Should I share what has been given freely to me or am I diluting the gift that is mine? In other words, if I tell her what I know, then she will know what she knows and what I know and then she may know twice as much as I know. I consider the options and decide to give her the answer. Then she asks for the second answer. This is now the proverbial "give an inch and they will take a mile." I whisper, "I'm not sure the first one is right so I can't be responsible for giving you two wrong answers."

She says, "That's okay. Crud, I won't get any right with or without your help."

I give her my homework. She copies it quickly before Sister comes back. The bell rings, and she stops to tell me her name is Janette, and thanks me for my help. She gives me a book she has just finished reading and says it is really good.

That night I ask Martina to look over my math homework. Half of them are wrong and she works with me until I think I might understand some of it. I show her the book Janette has given me and ask what she is reading. She says it is called *Her Brilliant Career* by Rachel Cook. She recommends it, but I don't care that much for that kind of book so I doubt I will ever read it.

Since she is now wrapped up in her book, I read the first page of my new book. It seems like a small thing, but this will change me and my love for books. I cannot put the book down. It is Friday and we get to have the lights on late, but I snuggle up by the window and continue reading by the light of the full moon even after the lights go out. At six the next morning I am almost finished. It has taken me longer than normal because I read and cry; then read and cry some more. My eyes are two red swollen wounds when I finish. And now I know the power of books and I want to read everything. I think I will never read anything as good as *Knock on Any Door* by Willard Motley. But of course, it's just the beginning.

Because Martina is a senior, she gets to go downtown on

Saturday. It must be in a group of course, but once they get there, they split up. Some want to go to the movie, some want to shop, some want to hang out at the local burger joint where they can flirt with boys, and my Martina wants to go to the library. She has a day student's library card so she can choose from a wide selection.

When she comes back, she has two new books. *The Last Curtsey* by Fiona McCarthy and another Eleanor Roosevelt biography. I am now interested in reading whatever books she has, and we are growing together in mind and spirit. Sunday after Mass, we spend the whole day reading and sharing quotes. We both like Eleanor's "You must do things you think you cannot do," and "The future belongs to those who believe in the beauty of their dreams."

Martina asks me, "What is your dream, Loretta?"

"I think I would like to be an Architect, but I would need more math, and I hate math. I'll see how well I do in the next three years. I would like to design buildings and houses, but I would need to go to college and I hate school. I do know that I will be the boss. I want to be in control. My life will be better when I am in charge."

I don't tell her the other thing I want is to have a family. Not children of my own necessarily, but I could be an aunt or a sister-in-law or something. Sunday dinners with a family like being at Miss Sarah's. That would be a dream come true.

A few nights later we are listening to Jerry Fox and I ask Martina, "What is a female fox called?"

"A vixen," she says.

"Holy Shit, Martina, that's it!"

"I really wish you wouldn't use that word, Loretta."

"Fine. Holy socks, then. The fox and the vixen. That's you."

"That's cute" She giggles.

"I'm serious, Martina. Call him tonight and request a song. He'll probably ask you what your name is, and you can say "I'm your vixen." Or however you work it in, it will knock him off his chair. And then flatter him on something he said."

"Even if I wanted to, I don't have a phone to call him and I would probably get tongue-tied and say it wrong. I can't."

"You must do the thing you think you cannot do. It's an omen, a sign from God or Eleanor. You must."

"But how?"

"I know. After bed check, wait for an hour then go down to Sister Joseph's office and use her phone. They are all asleep and they won't hear you. Worst case, one of them comes in. Just think of a good excuse, like you had a nightmare that your Uncle died, and you had to call to find out if it was true."

"Oh, I don't know. I'm not a good liar, and what if I get too nervous."

"If, 'ifs and buts' were candy and nuts, we'd all have a wonderful Christmas." First, don't trust anyone who can't tell a lie. Sometimes a lie is the kindest thing you can say. Second, I know this is your dream, so if you don't try, then how can you make your dream come true?"

"All right. Let me think about it. Now shut up."

"One last thing, Martina. While you are thinking about it, think about it working out just the way you want. Rehearse it over and over, and don't put any doubts in. Just imagine everything going perfectly."

Mentally exhausted, I fell asleep, but I woke up at 2:00 am when I heard Jerry Fox saying, "The Fox is going to play *Misty* for the Vixen. Goodnight and sweet dreams."

I look over and Martina is sitting on the edge of her bed – all smiles.

"You did it! Oh my God, tell me everything."

"I can't tell you everything, but we talked for three hours. It was heaven. I feel like I've known him all my life."

"Well, tell me something; anything."

"Okay, we talked about his life, his career, politics, religion. All the things you are not supposed to talk about. Go back to sleep. I'll tell you more tomorrow, and, oh, yeah, he asked me to call him again tomorrow night."

I fall back to sleep, and dream I am in a new house. I know it is my house and I love exploring all the rooms. I am rich.

21
Knock Me Down Shoes

The school experience has always been stressful for me. Latin, Algebra and even PE make me nervous and jerky. We don't actually have a gymnasium. It's just a room with hardwood floors, and we have a lay teacher who wants us to do ballet poses. Jesus H. Christ, who thinks up this stuff? Martina tells me not to say JC because that's a mortal sin. She says, "Cheese and crackers." I can't seem to remember that.

My kitchen duties are also hard, but I reward myself by eating all the leftovers I can shove into my mouth. Sister Diane doesn't like it and calls me a noob and a glutton when she catches me. She says I am supposed to confess my sins to Father on Saturday. Instead, I confess to Saint Martina and tell her "Sister Diane is a bitch."

"Don't say that word, Loretta. Now you have to confess that you also swore."

"What should I call her then?"

Martina hesitates and then says, "Call her a batch of cookies."

I say, "You're a batch of cookies." We both get the giggles. It makes my day to make her laugh.

She is talking to Jerry every night. She must be exhausted, so I cut her some slack. She has hidden her journal, so I still have no clue what they are talking about. She keeps her feelings pretty private, but she is smiling all the time.

Sister Joseph wants the boarders to put on 'Romeo and Juliet' for the day students and parents right after Christmas break. It is almost Thanksgiving and I know I will be staying, but Martina will be Greyhounding back to M&M's for turkey. She does not want to go.

I have already suggested that she try out for Juliet, but she doesn't want to do that either. The reason she doesn't want to go home is that she can't call Jerry, so I ask her, "What is more fearful, not to talk to Jerry or to put yourself in the spotlight? You can tell M&M that you must stay here and rehearse. There's your excuse. What's your choice?"

She tries out and, of course, she is Juliet. No one can compete with that face and that voice. I am just one of the rabble at the party, but I give it my all. My all also ends up painting scenery and building sets. Martina mocks me "Your first architecture job. Making your dream come true?"

About half the boarders stay at school for Thanksgiving. Most of them stay because they live too far away to travel just for a long weekend, and Christmas will be coming soon so they will see their families then. The nuns try to create a good time for us with turkey and all the trimmings, but most students are homesick so there "ain't no joy in Mudville."

We make crafty paper decorations to get ready for Christmas. We make Christmas cards like it's our job. Martina is the only one who is smiling. She spends hours with "Hair-do Helen" who plays Romeo. The reason we call her Hair-do Helen is because she has short, straight, slicked-down hair parted in the middle with lots of dandruff. We are not sure if it's a product she puts on that makes it stick to her head or if she just never washes it. We suspect it's the latter because she scratches her head and then licks her fingers. Yuck! I think she is also a boy or at least a boy wannabe. What a weirdo! And I'm not good enough to be at least a Montague?

It's my turn to mock Martina: "Oh, Romeo, kisseth me with thy scaly purple lips and rub thee dandruff upon my milky breasts, before I duth shit a brick and die."

"Home-ick" class is making all the costumes. I'm sure they will be used for many years, except for Romeo's hat which will surely be burned immediately after the performance by someone holding it with a ten-foot pole.

We make it through Thanksgiving and all the girls are excited to get out of here for Christmas vacation. Martina isn't, of course, but she says she has made a date to meet Jerry after the New Year. I look through her closet for something that isn't frumpy that she can wear, and it is obvious who has been picking out her clothes. I let her try on my most beloved black straight skirt. I cannot get my newly acquired ass into it anymore and it fits her like a glove. She is taller than me, so it hits her mid-knee. She fills out my white cotton blouse like it was made to be filled out. The only thing missing is a pair of "Joan Crawford, come fuck me shoes."

"Geez, Loretta don't use that word."

"Okay, Saint Martina. Let's hear it. What would you say instead of fuck? It's really the only word that fits."

"Well, say fudge, if you must intimate that word at all."

I begin to laugh. "Joan Crawford, come fudge me shoes?"

Now we are both laughing, and I can hardly get the words out. "Knock me down and fudge me shoes."

We are now doing the ugly face laugh where we are laughing out of control and our face is all screwed up and tears are coming out of our squinty eyes, and then I snort. That makes us laugh all the harder. Martina has flopped down on her bed holding her stomach, begging me to stop, but I can't, and neither can she until we lose our breath. We stop for a second and then begin again. It just gets funnier and funnier. It's a moment in time that I know I will always cherish, and it will always make me smile when the memory passes through my consciousness.

The day she leaves for Christmas break, I am bereft but cannot show it. I tell her to have a Merry Christmas and don't take Auntie M with her when she buys the fudging shoes. Neither one of us can laugh. I give her a package of cookies I confiscated from the kitchen with a Christmas card I made. She says she'll bring my present when she returns.

"Try not to get into any trouble while I'm gone."

"Right, like there's an opportunity for that."

We say our trite good-bye's bravely, but the feeling of love between us needs no words.

I am inconsolably lonely that night in our room. I turn on Martina's radio and Jerry Fox is soothing me to sleep as if Martina ordered it. Then I hear him say "This is for Lolo. Elvis' *Love Me Tender*." And that was my Christmas miracle.

22

A Black and White Christmas

The whole school is pretty deserted. I'm the only boarder and many of the nuns have gone somewhere. It's just a skeleton crew making the best of it.

Sister Joseph wants me to move closer to the nun's quarters, but I beg to stay in my room. She is in a generous mood and relents with a compromise. The three days before Christmas we will be on a silent retreat and I have to stay with the nuns until it is over on Christmas Day.

At first, I think this is going to be miserably hard, but it actually ends up being easy, and I find a new peace I didn't know I had. There are lots of kneeling, praying, rosary rituals and meditations. My new favorite nun, Sister Bertrum, tries to prepare me for the experience by teaching me how to clear the constant chatter in my mind by getting lost in the mantra of "Hail Mary, full of grace." She says when the "feeling" of Mary's grace fills me I can stop the mantra and be in the silence until I find my mind wandering and then begin the process again. I will work on it, but mostly I'm thinking of Martina and food because we are also fasting.

Christmas morning, I help Sister Diane make sticky buns for

a breakfast treat. While the dough is rising, we work on the turkey and dressing. By 8:00 am we are in the chapel for a quick Mass. Then Sister and I serve coffee or hot chocolate with the sticky buns in the leisure room where there are presents, and the festivities begin. I did not know what to expect. I mean, who knew nuns did presents?

The gifts are wrapped in groups with the same paper, mostly tissue paper of different colors tied up with long ribbons made from scraps left over from the material used for the costumes. There are no names saying who each group of packages is from.

I could tell that the handmade soap wrapped in green tissue paper with a red ribbon was Sister Mary Katherine's donation from home-ick. (I should probably stop calling it that). Red tissue paper with white ribbon contained six beautifully decorated Christmas cookies, obviously from Sister Diane. There were booklets, *Life is Worth Living* by Bishop Fulton Sheen, wrapped in white tissue paper with blue ribbon. Holy Spirit Prayer Candles were wrapped in blue tissue with gold ribbon. A beautiful box of blank note cards with a gold dove on the front with envelopes to match was wrapped in white tissue paper and gold ribbon. We all "oohed and aahed" over each gift. Then there were two big packages left, and Sister Joseph said: "Go ahead, Loretta, those are for you."

I carefully opened the first one and found a winter coat. It was red with a dark brown mouton fur collar. It was the best winter coat I ever had, and it caught me off guard. I was all choked up with gratitude. "Thank you, thank you so much. I love it!" I put it on and modeled it, pushing the collar up to my cheeks and then twirled. There were laughter and applause.

I unwrapped the last package and I gasped in horror, but hopefully, they thought it was joy. It was a blue corduroy jumper, empire style, A-line with pockets and a white, long-sleeve, cotton pullover turtleneck to go under it. I was speechless. I had no speech. It was f*ugly, but at least it was big enough and better than wearing my school uniform skirt everywhere. So, I overacted and pressed it to my chest and again thanked everyone.

Sister Joseph said, "It is really from your father, but we went shopping and picked everything out."

"Well, you sure did a great job. I love everything and this is really the best Christmas I can ever remember."

Sister Gretchen, our music teacher said, "Let's sing some Christmas carols." She went to the piano and we all followed, except Sister Diane who went to check on everything in the kitchen. I started to follow her, but she insisted I stay and sing. We sang for about a half hour until Father McDonough came to call. He asked us not to stop and he joined in. There is something special that happens with a joint sing along. It's like music is the language of the soul and it makes every cell in your body vibrate with joy.

Sister Diane came back in and announced that the turkey would be ready in half an hour. "We hope you will stay for dinner, Father."

"Well, I thought you'd never ask. Sister Diane is famous for her turkey and sausage dressing," he says. "I look forward to it every year."

"Loretta, you come and help me set the table. The other Sisters stood to help but she said, "No, you entertain Father. We can handle this, can't we Loretta?"

"We sure can, Sister." I went gladly and with a new appreciation for Sister Diane.

Dinner was preceded by Father's way too long prayer of thanks and a tribute to Baby Jesus followed by thanking Sister

Diane and all the Dominican Sisters and blah, blah, blah. *Oh, please God, make it stop. He is really pissing me off. Who does he think he is, barging in on our celebration and sucking up all the attention, and the stuffing to boot.*

Once we started eating, I thought maybe he would shut up, but he continued with what he must have thought were witty stories. All the Sisters laughed and encouraged him on and on.

When everyone was finished eating, Sister Diane asked me to help her serve the pumpkin pie and coffee. In the kitchen, while plating the pie I asked Sister, "Do you really think Father McDonough is all that entertaining? Because I think he is overstaying his welcome."

Sister continued putting cups on a tray and said, "Loretta, we are here to serve, and being a good hostess is also listening to your guests, even if you are not interested in everything they say."

I was losing respect for her even though I could see her point, but then after the pie was eaten, she said, "Father, would you like a piece of pie to go?"

I almost spit out my milk. I wanted to jump out of my chair and get on my hands and knees and bow at her feet repeatedly. Father took the hint and got up to leave, again thanking us all for a lovely evening.

Then he said, "Oh, I almost forgot your gifts." He pulled out an envelope and gave it to Sister Joseph. There were tickets for us all to see "South Pacific." All the Sisters were thanking him profusely and so was I. Sister Diane and I looked at each other with big smiles. A happy confluence of minds.

That evening we all watched "It's a Wonderful Life" on TV. There was not a dry eye in the room at the end. I took my presents back to my own room and got on my knees and thanked God for all my blessings.

The rest of the vacation was more fun than I ever imagined living with a bunch of nuns could be. "South Pacific" was wonderful, and we all had a very serious conversation about discrimination and how loving we are until taught otherwise.

We played charades one night – two teams of three. Each team made the topics for the other. It was really funny when Sister Joseph got the one that I put in: Elvis. She did a great impression. Guitar strumming and swivel hips brought the house down. I had guessed that I was the only one in the room who would even know who he was. Guess nuns are not as sheltered as I thought.

We watched a lot of Liberace and reruns of Bishop Fulton Sheen talks. I enjoyed both, but I would not admit it to anyone. We had some pretty deep conversations after watching the Bishop. I usually didn't contribute and just soaked it all up.

Everyday Sister Diane and I made casseroles to freeze, getting a jump on food for the new year when everyone returned. I made lots of biscuits to freeze. Sister said I was really a big help to her and getting to be a very good cook. She actually let me fix breakfast a couple of times for everyone, and gave me all the credit when the Sisters said it was good.

I told Sister Diane I was thinking of becoming a nun and asked her what she thought about that?

She surprised me by saying, "Take your time Loretta. If you think it would be easy and you don't have to deal with life like it is on the outside, I would tell you that you will have the same problems to work out in here as you would on the other side. Relationships are all the same. You have to give and forgive just as much. Some of the women here didn't even pick this vocation. It was forced upon them by parents or just circumstances. Anyway, just take your time. I don't want to talk you into or out of anything. You have to follow your heart. You will eventually know, and you won't have to ask for anyone's opinion."

We spent a quiet, prayerful New Year's Eve and a busy New Year's Day getting ready for students coming back in two days. The boarders would be back soon and I cannot wait to see Martina.

It is late the next evening when she arrives. I tried to stay awake but was startled when she turned on the lights. "Hey, you finally made it."

"Hi, Loretta. Sorry that I woke you." Then she starts laughing. "Sit up! I want to give you your presents."

"I'm up. I'm awake. Gimmy, gimmy."

"Have you been good while I was away?" She teased.

"Yes, yes, Saintly good. Nun good. No fun good."

"Okay then, I guess I'll give you the best present first." She hands me a small package. Not tiny but smaller than a shoe box.

I rip into it. It's a sizeable bottle of Clearasil. "Just what I wanted and needed. Thank you."

"All right, calm down. Here's something you probably will want to return, but I couldn't think of anything else."

The package was about the size of a pizza box, but beautifully wrapped. I opened it up and hey, it is a pizza box. What? There is lots of tissue to remove before I see the album. It's Elvis! I stand up and jump around the room hugging and kissing it. "Thank you, thank you, thank you! I love it."

"Do you want to see the knock me down shoes I bought?" She opens her suitcase and presents a pair of the highest stiletto heels I've ever seen."

"Holy shit, Martina! You weren't fudging around. These are so cool. Let me see you walk in them."

She slipped them on and walked like a model up and down

the room, pivoting back and forth.

"I practiced every day for two weeks. I even wore them out one day when Auntie M was gone and the sidewalks were dry. I didn't go too far because I didn't want to get them scuffed and I got some black shoe polish just in case."

"They are wonderful. When is your date with Jerry? And oh, by the way, thank you so much for the Elvis dedication the night you left."

"What?"

She pretends she doesn't know what I'm talking about.

"You know. *Love Me Tender*."

"Okay, you're right. Were you surprised? I hoped you would hear it, but you could have easily missed it too."

"Yes, I was surprised, and it was the best Christmas gift up until now." I kiss and hug my present again.

"So, what is new with you?" She asks.

"Nothing very exciting, except I went to see "South Pacific" with the nuns. They gave Christmas presents. We sang and played games like Charades and Sister Joseph did Elvis." I do my imitation of her doing Elvis and we crack up laughing.

"Oh yeah, and I made Honor Roll."

"Well, I guess you are not just a smartass anymore. Congratulations. I knew you could do it."

Martina gets her jammies on while I tell her about Father McDonough, Sister Diane, and my new coat. Snuggled under the covers, we turn off the light.

"I hope I can fall asleep. I'm kind of wired. Talk me to sleep or do you want to listen to Jerry?" We both vote for Jerry and fall asleep immediately.

The next day the whole Sienna Hall is buzzing with excitement. Boarders are all back and getting together to work on the play and catching up on everyone's vacation news.

23

A Star is Born

The rehearsal on the day before the performance is a disaster. People are forgetting their lines and not hitting their marks and the whole thing looks like a fiasco. Instead of rehearsing more, Sister tells everyone to get a good night's sleep. Right, like that's going to happen. That night I have to talk Martina off the ledge. She is pretty sure she will lay an egg right there on stage.

"I have all the confidence in the world that you will be wonderful, but what's the worst thing that could happen? You forget a line? So, you'll fake it. No one in the audience will know, and what the hell do you care anyway? You'll never see any of these people again. Just take a deep breath, say a prayer that Spirit will give you the words and break a leg."

She is practically hyperventilating, so I say, "Maybe this story will help you.

"One time we were sitting on Miss Sarah's front porch listening to a baseball game on the radio. After the game, there was an interview with one of the players who had hit a home run almost every time he was up to bat, so they asked him what his secret was? He said every night before he goes to sleep, he visualizes himself at bat. He feels the bat in his hands and his body in the perfect stance. In slow motion he sees the ball coming towards him and he steps into the ball and feels the perfect swing. As the ball connects, he hears the sound of the sweet spot hitting the bat and he knows he has hit the ball perfectly. He practices this scene over and over until he falls asleep. And that's his advice. Practice, practice and then mentally practice some more. Voila.

"Now, as you are falling asleep, imagine how beautiful you look on stage and rehearse your lines until they come out perfect and the audience is on their feet clapping and yelling *Bravo* all in your honor. It's that old thing from the Bible, 'As a man thinketh and so it is'."

Backstage the night of the play, we watch the auditorium filling up with schoolmates and parents. Sister has us form a circle and hold hands. She tells us she has seen some far less prepared disasters miraculously come together for the final performance, and she isn't worried about any of us tonight. She says a prayer and sends us to our places.

The curtain goes up, the lights come on and it is magic. Martina is beautiful and her words are a gift back to Shakespeare. Even Romeo is believable.

I hear actual sobs from the audience at the end. The audience is on their feet clapping. A few *Bravos* are in the air. The cast takes a bow and then Romeo comes forward and, finally, Martina steps forward and the applause is elevated. I have chills and tears in my own eyes watching her take a second bow. We all hurry to the hall to thank people for coming and take in the congratulations. I can see Martina glowing with an aura of new confidence around her.

Sister Joseph invites us all back to the leisure room for Chamomile tea and biscuits with ham. Now we are starving, and the mood is so joyful. I think I shall never be this happy again.

Martina and I continue to talk about it in our room for an

hour, and then she goes to call Jerry. I turn on the radio and wait for some acknowledgment that they are in communication. I don't have to wait very long when he says, "For Lolo here's Elvis: *I want you! I need you! I love you!*"

Our time in the spotlight is all too short. The next day as we tear down the set, there is a feeling of melancholy. Martina doesn't seem to mind. She has other things to look forward to.

The following Saturday, she has her first in-person date with Jerry. She spends hours getting ready. A little makeup, mostly my mascara and lipstick. She is not accustomed to using makeup, but it has enhanced her beauty without being obvious. She looks stunning in my skirt and blouse, and I tell her to wear my new red coat. She hides her stiletto heels in a bag so she can change into them as soon as she gets downtown.

I am on pins and needles all morning and afternoon until she returns at 4:00. When she walks through the door, I don't have to ask if it went well, because she is beaming.

"We are simpatico. We cannot stop talking or smiling at each other. I am in love. I love everything about him, and he feels the same way I'm sure. At least he says he loves my mind and the rest of me ain't so bad either. He makes me laugh and I even make him laugh. This is the best feeling in the world. No wonder they write songs and poetry about it."

She talks the rest of the day and night about him unless we are eating and the nuns are around. I'm getting a little tired of hearing how wonderful he is, but I am happy for her. I hope he is sincere. It would probably destroy her for life if he is playing her. For all that potential, she is still very fragile.

The love affair continues every night on the phone and every Saturday. She has gotten rather private again as to what they do on Saturday's, but knowing Martina I'm sure it's still very innocent. I ask her if he is a good kisser and she says, "I don't kiss and tell."

I say, "Smile if you've been kissed."

She laughs and gives me a wink.

All too soon it is April. I don't remember anything about February and March. April 4th is Martina's 18th birthday. Sister Diane and I bake a special cake for her and we make her favorite meal and sing Happy Birthday.

Easter is late this year. Good Friday is on the 13th. Around 3:00 pm, a black cloud covers the sun for an hour. The sun appears briefly before it sets. We pray the Stations of the Cross before Mass. Jesus says, "It is finished." We fast again that night. Maybe because it is Friday the 13th I have the willies.

Saturday morning, I help Sister make breakfast. It is light with tea and warm biscuits and pears. I don't see Martina at breakfast, but I suppose she is getting ready to go meet Jerry, although I didn't think there would be a Saturday outing for the seniors. But what do I know?

After we clean the kitchen, I head back to our room. She is not there, so I guess there is an outing today. At lunch, I notice many of the seniors who regularly go out on Saturday are still around, but I don't think anything of it.

At 5:00 we are called to Chapel and Martina hasn't shown up. Now I am worried. When I pass Sister Joseph on the way to confession, she stops me and asks if I have seen Martina?

"No Sister, I was hoping she was with you."

On the way back from Mass, I tell Sister I am worried. "What should we do?" She tells me she has handled it and I should go to dinner. How the hell am I supposed to eat now? But I do manage. I go to my room and wait for some word from somebody, but nothing. I think when everyone has gone to sleep, I will call Jerry.

I turn on the radio. *It's Only Make Believe* by Conway Twitty is playing. I like this song. Conway sounds a lot like Elvis. When it is over, I hear Jerry say "This is the Fox, and then I hear that unmistakable voice say "and this is the Vixen. From the Foxes Den, here is Paul Anka: *I'm Just a Lonely Boy."*

"HOLY SHIT!" It's about to hit the fan. For the next hour, people are calling in and asking about the Vixen. They don't really respond with anything definitive, but he says things like "The Fox must have his Vixen," and then she says, ". . . and the Vixen must have her Fox."

There is plenty of witty banter and innuendo. Men call in wanting to know if the Vixen is as "foxy" as she sounds, and women call in and say they think she should be called "The Voice." She is, by every indication, an overnight success. At 10:00 on the nose, she says, "I want to say good-night to my best friend, Lolo, who loves Elvis. This one is for you dear friend."

I resist the urge to go to Sister's office and call the station. I'm torn between being angry that she left without a word, grieving that she is gone, and feeling happy that she is living a dream that I had for her before she did.

By Monday, all anyone can talk about is the Vixen, and is it Martina? Students are looking for her in every classroom, so by the end of the day, it is confirmed. Sienna Hall is the last to know because no one listens to the radio here. Now girls who never talked to me before are trying to get information from me and be my friends. I tell them I'm not at liberty to talk about it.

Sister Joseph comes into my room and says I can now have the bed and room to myself, plus Martina is bestowing all her worldly possessions to me. Sister sits on the bed and asks me if I was aware of all of this? I tell her I didn't have any idea and that I'm mad that she didn't say good-bye. Then she asks if I'm okay or do I want to talk about it. I say "No, I've dealt with worse. I'll be fine but thank you for asking." We leave it at that.

By May 15th, Janette tells me Martina's picture along with Jerry Fox is plastered on billboards all over town. "You two were good friends, weren't you?"

"Yes, we were roommates. Do you listen to their show?"

"I do. They are pretty funny sometimes and I like the music they play."

"If you listen at 10:00, she always dedicates an Elvis song to Lolo. That's my nickname."

"No kidding? That is so cool."

"You're cool," I respond.

"What?"

"Never mind."

We are getting ready for finals and everyone is excited about summer vacation. I am dreading it.

On the 20th, Sister Joseph calls me into her office over the loudspeaker. I figure that can't be good. I take my time strolling down the hall trying to think of what this could be about. As I enter her office, she is sitting at her desk with her angry cherub face. I smile a fearless innocent smile at it. She says "Good afternoon Loretta."

"Good afternoon, Sister."

She returns my smile and says, "Aren't you going to say hello to your friend?"

I turn around and there is Martina.

"Martina!" Before I can even think, I am bear hugging her.

Sister gets up and says, "I'll give you some time together."

"I'm so sorry, Loretta, that I couldn't tell you everything. I know I could trust you, but I just couldn't tell you. I hope you forgive me because you really are my best friend and I want you to know I owe you everything. I wouldn't be married to Jerry or be on the radio without you pushing me and giving me the confidence that I needed to take every step."

I respond, "I feel like *I* owe *you* everything. I made honor roll again and it is all because of you. I actually had a wonderful year all because of you." I want to say more but my voice is cracking, and holding the tears back is causing the growing lump in my throat to shoot a pain into my jaw, but that is nothing compared to the stabbing pain in my heart.

Martina explains that she has convinced Sister Joseph to let her take her finals and get her diploma so she can continue her education. She plans on working and going to school. "I still want to teach someday."

Sister Joseph comes back into her office so I know it is over and we must say goodbye – maybe forever, even though Martina says she will keep in touch I know from past experience with Sandy that this might be the end. I think I have regained my composure, so I ask one last question. "How did Aunty M take this news?"

"Like a batch of cookies." Martina laughs and the floodgates open for me. There is no holding back now. I hug her and whisper through gasps and sobs, "I love you." It feels like this is the first time I have ever said those words.

"I love you too, Lolo."

I think it is the first time I have ever heard those words.

24
Summer Vacation 1959

Karen, a sophomore from school, was my traveling companion for the first leg of the train ride. She would be departing in Chicago, and I would change trains and finish the last many hours on my own. In the taxi on the way to the train station, we talked briefly about Sienna Hall and what she would be doing the rest of the summer. She did not ask me anything, but I felt it was my duty to keep the conversation going to avoid any awkward silences. When we passed a billboard with Martina's picture, I said, "That's quite a success story to tell your family about."

"I don't consider being a disc jockey much of a success story. Certainly, my family wouldn't be impressed."

Our conversation ended there. She was treading on hallowed ground. We ended up sitting across from one another on the train, so I took out my book and decided to ignore this "batch of cookies."

At our first stop, there were two young men who boarded the train and sat in the two vacant seats. They began to pursue Karen like she was the last chick on earth. The loud minutia and feeble joking by the boys followed by Karen's incessant giggling kept me from focusing on my book. I was riding the rail between curiosity and contemplating murder.

Karen is not that attractive and about as deep as a shot glass, yet these two hormones were twisting themselves into knots competing for her attention. I thought the attraction might have been when she said she lived on the North Shore in Chicago. Apparently, that is a very desirable neighborhood as it seemed to pique their interest immediately. For the next hundred hours – well it seemed like a hundred – I was not even given an acknowledgment that I existed in their presence. I excused myself to go to the dining car and attempted to gracefully climb over their feet blocking my path. Apparently, I was invisible.

In the dining car, I bless my turkey club and thank God I'm not a bitch anymore, like Karen. You never know what you do that will have a significant influence on someone else. Like the "Baby Huey" comment, it's a lesson that taught me kindness. I wonder how Donna is doing?

When I am finished with my sandwich, I begin to read my book at the table. The waiter comes by and says I have to order something else or leave. I don't have that much money, so I decided to go back to the bane of my existence, but I search for a vacant seat along the way. My fate seems to be sealed for the next three hours. Or is it?

I choose not to be their minion. When they again refuse to move their feet to make a path for me, I feign clumsiness in getting to my seat. I step on every foot and stumble hard into a lap with a closed fist. A sound like a cat in a fan belt fills the area as he pushes me off and cups his nuts. I am propelled across to the other seat where I land in the other lap, oh, so gracefully, but I do manage to kick him in the shin. All the while, I'm apologizing profusely. "Sorry, sorry, whoops. Guess I'm the triple threat; trip, stumble and fall." Tee hee.

Karen is rubbing her foot, and I can tell by her glare that she hates my guts. The three of them hobble to the dining room and

I stretch out and read my book. I don't see them until we depart the train in Chicago. I wave enthusiastically and yell, "Bye Karen. See you in September. Be good."

The next part of the journey is uneventful, and I have no qualms about the first part. I finish my book. I watch out the window and eventually fall asleep. The conductor wakes me up to tell me the next stop is Rockton. It is 8:00 at night and I look around to see if anyone is there to pick me up. I call a cab to take me home.

25
Tubby Comes Home

The house is dark, but the door is not locked as usual. I don't think anyone has ever locked their door in Rockton. The house looks the same, smells the same and feels the same. My room is like a familiar happy dream. "Hello, my darling Elvis. I've missed you."

Back downstairs, I search the kitchen for something to eat. Old Mother Hubbard went to the cupboard, but here, there wasn't even a bone. I have a bowl of cereal. I think the cereal is at least eight months old. Home, sweet home. As I rinse out the bowl, I see car lights coming into the driveway.

Ughhhh, I take a deep breath and brace myself. I am determined to give this relationship another go. Give and forgive.

He lumbers through the door and says with a growl. "So, you're back."

"Yes, I just got back a little bit ago. The place looks the same." I use my most cheerful voice.

"Grunt." His effort at a conversation, I guess.

"I made Honor Roll." I'm still optimistic.

"You're fat."

The turpitude of my homecoming. What did I expect?

"Yeah, I was working in the kitchen at school. Temptation,

ya know? I need to buy some new clothes."

"Well, you better get a job then."

And that was it. The worst was over. He walked away.

I slept in the next morning until the sun shining through my window upon my face made it impossible to avoid the rest of the day. As I ate the last of the cereal and milk, I scanned the 'help wanted' section of the paper.

Jobs were divided into men wanted and women wanted. Apparently, women were not capable of delivering milk or were not qualified to do anything that paid a decent wage. I could be a car hop at A&W Root Beer, provided I had experience. I might be hired as a concession worker at the Drive-In Theater, but that would require riding my bike there and back at night which is a pretty long haul. Seems I am not old enough or experienced enough for even the lowest of women's work. Oh, wait, a Mother's Helper. I can do that.

I call the number and talk the lady into an interview even though she wanted someone a little older than fifteen. She said she was looking for a live-in for the summer and I said that would be perfect for me, so with that, she invited me to come over to talk.

I take all the money on "its" (now *he* is just an *it)* dresser and ride Blue Blaze to the Goodwill store where I search for a pair of jeans and a man's white shirt. As I turn down one aisle. I almost bump head-on into Margaret. She looks beautiful and thin as ever, but her eyes widen in fright or shock when she sees me. She has her arms full of stuff.

We stare into each other's eyes and look for answers, but apparently, there are none. I break the silence and say 'Hey, Margaret." She drops everything and high-tails it out of the store without a word. It was truly weird on both of our parts.

I look through the pile she left behind, and it gets weirder.

It's just an assortment of scarves and gloves. Why on earth would anyone need so many scarves and gloves? I did find a cute scarf in the pile to tie around my ponytail, so "Thanks, Margaret."

Back home, I cut the jeans into Bermuda length shorts and tie the shirt bottom at my waist. I put on my white tennis shoes, bobby socks with the comb in the side and put my hair in a ponytail with my new scarf. I think I look like an all-American girl who could be trusted with someone's kids.

I hop on my trusty "Blue Blaze" and peddle over to a very ritzy part of town and find the address. I'm looking at the numbers on a mailbox in front of a veritable mansion. I feel a little less confident now and wish I had a nice sundress to wear, but I find the courage to knock on the door and confront my fears.

26

Perfect Wife; Perfect Life

Mrs. Murphy is a carbon copy of every housewife on TV selling refrigerators. Short blonde hair, brown eyes, pink lips, tiny ass sporting a pair of toreador pants, and flats.

"Hi, I'm Loretta. Thank you for inviting me over to meet with you."

"Come in Loretta. I was just going to have a glass of lemonade. Would you like a glass?"

"Oh, that would be lovely. Thank you." Wow, I think we even sound like a TV show.

I follow her into the kitchen which is spectacular, and I tell her so. She thanks me and asks me if I cook very much?

"I am a really good cook and baker. I just got home from Sacred Heart Academy. It's a finishing school, and I was very active in the kitchen learning from the best. I've always had a great interest in cooking. Wait until you taste my tuna noodle casserole."

"So, you are Catholic? So are we," she says with new interest.

"Oh yes, I think you not only get the best education, but the Sisters really teach you respect and how to be of service. You know, good manners are so important." Oh shit, I should have said something about religious training. I'll get to it somewhere along the line.

She is smiling now, and we walk back into the living room and sit down. The sofa is covered in plastic and makes a squishy sound when I sit on it.

"You said you have three girls. How old are they?"

"Judy is 8, Joanie is 7 and Julie is 5."

It appears she has figured out the rhythm system at last.

"Judy, Joanie, and Julie – how cute. What activities are they involved in?"

"Well, that's the thing. With three small children and a house to keep, plus all my volunteer demands, I haven't been able to devote time to a lot of activities that I would like to have the girl's experience. My husband is Vice President of the First National Bank and that requires a significant amount of entertaining and socializing on my part also."

"Wow, I can see that you could use a lot of help. I'm in awe of all you are doing so beautifully with all your responsibilities."

"Thank you, Loretta. Sometimes a housewife's work is easily dismissed as though I'm sitting around and watching soap operas all day."

"I am willing to do whatever you need, but for starters, I would like to take the girls to the park often to make sure they get exercise and fresh air. I like books, so I would like to take them to the library to get them involved in reading. If there are any school subjects that they need a little help with, I can make up games so they don't even know they are learning while having fun. And of course, I can get them to help bake, and I would love to make dinner whenever you need help. I make a lot of great casseroles, not just tuna." I give a slight laugh.

"That sounds wonderful, Loretta. Just getting the girls out of the house so I can focus on other things would be a big help. I love everything you have suggested, but are you sure you don't mind living in? I mean wouldn't this interfere with your social life? And what do your parents think?"

"Gosh no, Mrs. Murphy. My mother has passed, and Dad is very busy with his business. My social life is back at boarding school. I'm much more interested in reading and studying. I plan on being an architect. I do enjoy movies though, but I bet your girls would enjoy them also, right?"

"They do love movies. And please call me Lois."

"How about if we compromise, and I'll call you Mrs. M or just Ma'am?"

"Mrs. M would be perfect. Do you have a reference that I could call so I can tell my husband I did my due diligence? And when would you be able to start?"

"You can call Mrs. Sarah Johnson for a reference. She has known me all my life. By the way, if you need someone to come and clean your house and cook some delicious fried chicken, I can be her reference. I can start tomorrow or even today, but first I would like to meet the girls and make sure we are a good fit."

"Oh, yes, of course. I guess we should also discuss your salary. Along with room and board, I was thinking $25 a week. Would that be enough for you?

I hesitate even though I would have accepted less, but I want her to know that I know she is getting a hell of a deal. Finally, I negotiate, "I think that would be fine if I can have Sunday off."

"It's a deal." She offers me her hand to shake. "Let me get the girls up here." She goes to the kitchen and opens a door to a lower level and commands them upstairs. I stand up quickly when she is gone because I'm stuck on the plastic and it is making me sweat.

They come into the living room like three little ducks in a row. Mrs. M introduces each one. They are quiet and shy when I tell them my name is Loretta but my friends call me Lolo.

"Would it be okay if we went for a walk around the block and searched for hidden treasure?"

They reply in unison, "Yes!" And off we go. I know kids just want someone to pay attention to them. We become fast friends, except for Julie who is more reticent. We look for rocks and bugs and anything they think is a treasure while we talk about the fun things we could do together. I think this is the first time in their little lives that they have walked around the block, so it is our first adventure.

Back home, the girls are all chattering at once about our travels: the frog we saw and the treasures they found; a rock that looks like a heart and one that Julie thinks is beautiful. Mrs. M is pleased that everyone has found what they were looking for, especially me.

We all take a tour of the house and I see where I am going to be sleeping. Julie is excited because I am sharing a room with her. There is a trundle bed in Julie's room that will be just fine. Each girl's bedroom is in perfect order. The lower level is where all the toys are so there is never a mess upstairs. The laundry room and furnace are also down there. A few very small windows barely let in enough light to call them windows, so it is rather gloomy. No wonder the girls were so excited to get out.

The girls hear a car pull in and they begin to jump up and down. "Daddy's home! Come on Lolo." They pull me up the stairs and out the door. We run to the tall handsome man who is looking at Blue Blaze.

"Daddy, this is Lolo, she is going to live with us all summer." Judy is delivering the good news.

"Hello, Lolo. Welcome. I see you have made some new friends."

"Nice to meet you, Mr. Murphy. Yes, we are having fun already. I should be going now and let you relax, but I'll be back to stay in the morning. Is eight o'clock okay?"

Mrs. M is standing by her man, and she nods her head yes.

"I think before you leave, I should pump up your tires. They are almost flat. It must have been a tough ride over here."

"Gosh, I thought it was just me, out of practice." We all laugh. It feels like the perfect family, and I am now part of it.

The ride back home is a breeze. I'm starving, so I stop and get a burger and fries at the Tasty Freeze. I want a hot fudge sundae but I'm out of money, so I consider this the first day of my new diet.

27

Summer Time

All of June is like living the childhood I never had, and I get to do all my favorite childhood things with my three new friends. We play jacks, jump rope – including double-dutch – play hopscotch, and spend days at the park. We take the bus to the movies and the library. The girls think it is a big deal. Each girl gets to check out two books, and I get one that we read together at bedtime. The first one we get is *Heidi*. For the next two weeks, Julie insists on having her hair braided and wants to be called Heidi.

The second book I choose is *Charlotte's Web*. I pick that one because of Martina. I want to tell her that I have my own M&M now, but they are super nice, not controlling at all.

After lunch, we have a ritual I call "Imagine Time." We all lay on the floor in Judy or Joanie's room and we close our eyes and imagine different stories. We imagine places we would like to go and things we would like to do or be. One of the girls will start it and then they want me to finish it. They end up taking a nap and they don't even know it's nap time.

This is my time to help Mrs. M with whatever she needs. If she isn't home, I make a casserole and put it in the fridge for dinner or make a salad or the lemonade or ice tea for the afternoon. The girls like Kool-Aid so I make that just for them.

On Mondays, Miss Sarah shows up and makes fried chicken that she puts in the oven on low with a damp tea towel over it so it's still moist and juicy at dinner. She cleans the house, and if Mrs. M is gone, we get to talk while I help her dust. We have deep conversations about life, and I realize most of whatever wisdom I ever told Martina has come from Miss Sarah.

She keeps me up on what Ruth and Marilee are up to. I try not to act overly interested in Tyrone, but of course, that is who I really want to hear about. I ask her if he has a girlfriend, and she says no one he is serious about and she is happy about that. So am I. She thanks me for getting her this job, but I am the thankful one.

Every morning I make biscuits for breakfast. Mr. M is a big fan, and I want to please him. Mrs. M has a dishwasher, but she doesn't like to use it. For a while, I washed the dishes and she either dried them or they dried in a rack on the counter. Then, I put them away while the girls were taking their nap.

Finally, I told her to not worry about the dishes, that I will do them all. All I do is wash and rinse them and then put them on the rack of the dishwasher to dry so they are off the counter. I do the same thing with the dinner dishes. The girls set the table so it is easier for them to reach the dishes in the dishwasher. Judy gets the glasses, Joanie gets the plates and Julie gets the silverware. This becomes part of their chores to secure a weekly allowance. Mrs. M loves this system because she cannot stand anything on the counters and has never taken the time to teach the girls how to do anything.

Each week the girls and I plan our days and how we will spend our weekly fun allowance. It's all very democratic. We discuss the activities we want to do that cost money and make a list on their blackboard. We have to budget money for the bus, snacks, movies and special things like going to the roller rink and any supplies that we might want. I inflate the price of most things so they really have to prioritize and agree. If there isn't an agreement, then we can't do anything. I say that's the rule. Sister Diane says, "Cooperation is the first lesson in a peaceful life."

By July, my Bermuda cutoff jeans are so loose I need a go to the Goodwill again and get the next size down. I cut them off, but this time a little shorter. Short shorts are the rage because of the summer song "Short Shorts." The one thing I liked about being fat was that my boobs were big, too. They have not shrunk with this new weight loss, so I hope I have just grown into them at last.

The Fourth of July we take a picnic basket of Miss Sarah's chicken down to the lakefront and sit on the grass and wait for the fireworks. Mr. and Mrs. M lay on a blanket while the girls and I go play on the swing sets. As dusk sets in, we open the basket and devour the chicken and biscuits. The fireworks are magical, and I look at the girls' faces all filled with awe. I am overcome with pride when the speakers blast the *Star Spangled Banner*. We all stand with our hands over our hearts. America! America! I love my life. I love my girls.

28
Daddy's Home!

Each of the girls has her own distinctive personality. Judy is very serious. Joanie is a chatterbox who sometimes needs to be shut down for everyone's sanity. I have explained to her about over-talking and we have come up with a phrase that she understands. When I say it, she stops talking for about five minutes, which is all she can manage. The phrase is "Give it a rest." There are no hard feelings when I say this to her. She just knows it means to take a quick nap with your words. Julie is a sponge, soaking up everything each of us says. Nothing gets by her, and we are all conscious to not say anything we don't want to be repeated. "Little pitchers have big ears."

One day at the library, Joanie spots a portrait of Albert Einstein with his tongue stuck out, and below the picture is a quote: "Imagination is more important than knowledge."

Julie wants to know who that is and why is he doing that? The four of us stand before the picture and I ask Judy if she knows who he is? She does not, so I explain, "Albert Einstein was a scientist and the smartest man in the whole world. He understood everything about everything in the universe, and yet he says imagination is even more important than all the knowledge he possessed. That's why books are so important and spending time doing 'imagine time' is good for us to do every day. And the reason he is making that funny face is to remind us to have fun and enjoy life."

The dynamics of a family are very interesting to me. I observe how Mrs. M conducts herself on the phone, with her bridge group when they meet at her house, her interactions with Mr. M and, of course, with her children. Everything seems to revolve around Mr. M. It's a big deal when he comes home. Like now, we can all start living. At the dinner table, he is King and holds court. How was his day? How is he feeling? What does he like for dinner? He pontificates about the news of the day or a neighbor or whatever subject he chooses. He is the type that if asked what time it is, he will tell you how to build a watch.

When Mrs. M wants to talk about her day, she simply tells it in a question that he can then expound upon or solve the problem even though there never was one. She has to be very careful about what she tells him or a long lecture will ensue. I find myself fawning over him also, and I don't even understand why I do it. It seems to be the group mentality.

Shortly after talking about Einstein at the library, we spend a full afternoon practicing riding Blue Blaze. At dinner, Judy asks her father if she could have a two-wheeler like Blaze. Uh, oh. Her question sparks a long diatribe on the appropriate age, the dangers, and maintenance of bicycles. Five or ten minutes into it, Julie says "Give it a rest, Einstein."

I swear Kool-Aid shot out of Judy's nose and we all laughed hysterically. Even Mrs. M couldn't stop laughing, but after we saw the look on Mr. M's face, we all calm down quickly. He tells Julie that she is rude, and she cannot have dessert. The table becomes very quiet and uncomfortable. Julie's eyes fill with tears and her lip quivers. She weeps silently and it is painful for us to watch, but we are powerless. I stare at my plate, but I cannot take another bite of food or I will throw up.

Finally, Julie asks if she can go to her room. She is excused and runs upstairs. Mr. M pushes his plate away in disgust and gets up in a huff. I just want to go up and comfort Julie, but instead, I clear the table and stay in the kitchen. I am grateful that I must do the dishes while everyone else goes into the living room and pretend to watch TV.

I am planning on sneaking Julie a piece of cake at some point, but I have to wait until the cake is served to the rest. I go to check on Julie before going into the living room to join the rest of the family. She has cried herself to sleep. She looks like the innocent little angel that she is. I can't remember ever being that sweet or that innocent.

I wonder how these slings and arrows to her self-esteem will affect her later in her life? God, I feel like this is my fault. They must have been crazy to put me in charge. Does Mr. M feel guilty also? Or did this make him feel like a big man? I lay down and cuddle with Julie.

Mrs. M comes up and whispers that it's time for cake. I tell her she can keep the goddamn cake. I see that she is shocked, and I am glad. At this point, I don't care if I get fired. Someone around here needs to speak up.

The next day there is no mention of last night, but I do not make biscuits. No dessert for Julie; no biscuits for Mr. M. This is Mrs. M's bridge day out of the house, so we go to the movies and then to the A&W for root beer floats. It's Friday, so I make grilled cheese sandwiches and tomato soup for dinner because I know it is Julie's favorite and, of course, there is chocolate cake for dessert.

Everyone is quiet during dinner. It is up to Mr. M to carry on his conversation that no one else gives a shit about. At this point, everyone knows what their role is in the family. Mrs. M is there to be the supporter and enabler, the girls are there to be seen and not heard, and I am there to make everyone's role a little easier. Mr. M is the boss, the king, the power, the omniscient giver of life and the executioner. We all bow down.

Tonight, he is the benevolent giver as he declares, "Let's all go watch *Rin Tin Tin* and eat our dessert in the living room. Lolo, would you serve the cake?" Cheers all around.

"Thank you, Daddy."

Now that we are all on the same page or Daddy's page, the rest of July flows along smoothly. I choose *Little Women* as our next book. We avoid looking at the picture of Einstein.

29

A Driving Lesson

August is here, and I am conscious of enjoying the last month of my freedom, so each day holds a special promise. I am now able to fit into all my old clothes, so my closet feels abundant and so do my boobs. I admire my figure in the mirror. This is how I always imagined it would look. Even my face looks better with the help of a good tan and Clearasil. I think I am pretty cute. I imagine those two hormones on the train would be focused on me now, instead of Karen. Maybe I'll have a chance to prove it on the trip back.

Most of all, I am cherishing every moment with the girls. It will be hard to leave them in three weeks, but I am positive Mrs. M will ask me to come back next summer. I love this family and I am even back on the love train with Mr. M. I realize it is five women to one man, so he is probably just displaying his masculinity like a big ape. I'm sure under all that chest pounding, there is a teddy bear.

Mrs. M told us at breakfast that on Friday we are all leaving to go to a summer cabin on a lake for a ten-day vacation. The girls are looking forward to it and tell me all about the cabin and the lake where they go every summer. There will be fishing, boating, swimming, picnics, and adventures in the woods. It sounds like great fun and my first vacation ever.

We pick up books at the library to read in the car, and I get *The Swiss Family Robinson* for us to read together at night. It sounds like we will imagine ourselves roughing it just like the Robinson family. I take Blue Blaze home and pick up my bathing suit and a couple additional tops for the trip. I cut my jean shorts very short. I kiss Elvis good-bye and head back to M&M's.

The car ride is fun even though we are really packed into the station wagon. We play card games, read our books, and listen to music on the radio. Thankfully Mr. M. likes the new music, and the station he chooses plays lots of Elvis. I am nostalgic because Elvis is in the Army now and I don't want anyone to forget him – as if we ever could.

We arrive at the cabin around 2:00 pm and get the car unpacked. The girls and I will be in one bedroom next to M&M's. There is one big living room and kitchen combination with one bathroom and a really nice front porch that overlooks the lake. I see there is also a dock and a rowboat with a motor for fishing. A short walk takes you to a Victorian style house that includes a restaurant and a bar with a pool table and jukebox. About a mile away is a general store that also sells gasoline and bait.

After everything is unloaded and put away, the girls and I put on our bathing suits and we head to the dock. I put my suit on in the bathroom for modesty reasons. I don't know what is appropriate for girls of their ages. Judy and Joanie know how to swim, but Julie does not, so I spend a lot of time teaching her. It reminds me of the times Tyrone taught me to swim in the pond behind the church. She catches on quickly, but I keep a close eye on them all. There is a nice sandy beach and the water is only waist high to the end of the dock. We stay in the water until 5:00 pm when we are called to get ready for dinner.

We are going to the restaurant and Mrs. M says it is casual so I put my jean shorts on over my bathing suit and the girls slip a pair of shorts over theirs. Dinner is served between 4 and 6; after that, you are on your own or you can get a hot dog at the bar. We end up doing that more often than the restaurant. PB&J is usually the easy choice for lunch in the cabin.

The first night after dinner the girls and I play some cards for a while, but by 8:00 p.m., Julie is sleeping at the table and Judy and Joanie are ready for bed also. The sun and water make good bedfellows. M&M go to the bar. I wake up when I hear them come in. Mrs. M is giggling and I hear their lovemaking noises. She keeps shushing him, but he seems not to pay any attention. I hope the girls don't wake up. Finally, it is over and I try in vain to fall back asleep.

The daily routine varies only with boating, fishing, and hot dogs. At the end of four days, Mrs. M makes a run to the general store for supplies and Mr. M goes swimming with us. He is pretty playful with the girls and even insists that I get on his shoulders as he wades out past the dock. When he ducks under water to release me, he accidentally grabs my boob. I'm really embarrassed and I'm sure he is too.

A few days later a friend of his shows up and they talk about going fishing. He sends Mrs. M to the store for beer and the girls want to go with her. I am in my bedroom when I hear the two men come into M&M's room. There is a slight gap in the horizontal boards in the wall between the two bedrooms, and for whatever reason, I peek through. I watch the two men undress and get into their bathing suits. Mr. M is facing my way and he takes his time getting into his suit. The men seem more interested in conversation than getting dressed. I am surprised that they are not self-conscious about being naked in front of one another. I don't think this would ever happen with girls.

When Mrs. M comes back with the beer, Mr. M puts it in a cooler and the two men take off in the boat to fish. We girls follow them to the dock with our blanket and books. We swim for a while and then we get into inner tubes and float around and have "imagine time" with Mrs. M included. There are silly stories and laughter and then bumper tubes.

Finally, worn out by the sun, we move our blanket into the shade and lay back and look at the clouds and point out shapes. "Oh, look, there's a sailboat. That one over there looks like a witch. No, it's an angel." I never want this moment to end. I want the smell of the lake and the sand and my girls forever embedded in my memory.

I wake up to the sound of the boat motor coming into the dock. Mrs. M is already down there helping to tie up the boat. The men are smiling and showing off their catch – a whole string of crappie. They whoop and yell like kids who just won first prize. Mrs. M is joining in. The girls wake up and we all walk down to the end of the dock to get a better look. Mr. M says there will be a fish fry tonight. I have never had fish to eat so I guess I'm happy.

Mr. M's friend Bill stays for dinner and we eat outside at the picnic table. The fish is okay, but I'm not a fan of the fish bones. Julie whispers to me that she doesn't like her fish. The house rule is everyone must clean their plate, so to avoid trouble, I sneak pieces of fish off her plate and eat it even though I am having trouble getting it all down. It reminds me of Miss Sarah and how she never made me eat anything I didn't like. I hope Mr. M and his friend do not go fishing again.

The grown-ups go to the bar, and we watch TV even though there is only one channel that comes in halfway decent. I think we are watching *Dragnet*, but there is so much interference it is hard to tell. We give it up and go to bed and I read some more of *The Swiss Family Robinson*. Judy thinks we could build a fort in the woods tomorrow.

After breakfast, the girls insist that we try to build a fort, so we pretend we are shipwrecked and we play in the woods all day. I must admit it was fun. We get too hot to continue and cool off in the lake. Mrs. M cooks burgers on the grill and we eat at the picnic table again. We finish eating and I clean up the dishes while the family sits on the front porch and listen to the radio.

When I come out, Mr. M says, "Oh, I still have Bill's license so I'm going to take a run over to drop it off. Why don't you come with, Lolo, and I'll give you a driving lesson?"

"What?" This takes me by surprise. Where did that come from?

"Well, next summer you can take the girls in the car instead of the bus. You do want to learn to drive, right?"

"Sure. That would be cool." I'm excited about the prospect of driving around in a car. "I'll go change out of my bathing suit."

"You don't need to change, we won't be gone long." He gets up and grabs his keys and we are off. It only takes about ten minutes to get to Bill's cabin and Mr. M tells me to wait in the car and he'll be right back.

When he comes back, he tells me to get in the driver's seat. He tells me about the proper hand positioning – ten and two – and to only use one foot for the gas and the brake. I step on the gas slowly and we drive down the road. He is still telling me all the ins and outs of driving like this takes some kind of genius. It really couldn't be simpler. It's certainly not as hard as learning to ride a bicycle.

"Turn down this road. There's no traffic down here."

I make the turn, and he pats my bare leg. "You're doing just fine." But he doesn't remove his hand.

The pat begins to be more of a gentle rub and further up my leg. I am getting very nervous now and afraid of what this means. His hand is now moving to my inner thigh. I step on the gas as his fingers slip under my bathing suit and between my legs. I slam on the brake.

"I, I, don't want to drive anymore. You drive."

"Okay honey, slide over." He still has his hand between my legs and the more I squirm, the more he fingers me. "I'll get out and come around."

I am in a panic now. What should I do? Why is he doing this? I open the car door and jump out. He gets out of his side and meets me halfway. He pushes me against the car and pulls my bathing suit down and squeezes my breast and tries to kiss me.

"No, no, Mr. M. Please don't. Let's go."

He puts his fingers under my nose and says, "smell it. Lick it." He pushes his finger in my mouth.

"You know you want it. I know you were watching me get undressed. Did you like what you saw? Did you like how big my cock is?"

"No. I'm sorry. Please let's go. Please stop."

"Yes, that's right. It isn't any fun unless somebody is saying no." He has pushed my suit to the ground and has his fingers inside me. "Here, look at my cock. It wants to feel your hot little pussy all around it." He shoves it in me. "Take it all in, Bitch. You know you want it. Your pussy is wet and loves my cock."

I am whimpering, but he doesn't know anything except his lust. He pulls it out and jerks off on my belly. I think he is finished, and we can leave and forget it ever happened, but he rubs his hand around on my belly and his cum. He is sucking on my tit and has his fingers inside me again. I don't want to enjoy any of this, but I feel my clit getting hard and then I can't control my breath and I convulse in shame.

"That's my girl. That's my girl. Your pussy is hot and wet. You love it. Now put my cock in your mouth and suck all the juice out of it." He pushes me down and forces me to take it in my mouth. "Yes, yes, suck it, lick it, baby." He cums in my mouth and he groans long and loud.

He pulls me up and helps me get my bathing suit back on. He acts like this is all normal behavior. Nothing to see here. I am wobbly and incapable of dressing myself. In a daze, I get in the car.

Driving back to the cabin, he looks over at me and pats my knee. It makes me jump. "You and I have a special love, Lolo. I have wanted you as much as you have wanted me from the very first day we saw each other. Tonight was wonderful, and I know you liked it too."

I didn't say anything. What could I say? Did I like some of it? Did I want this to happen? No. I don't think I wanted this to happen. This ruins everything. We just burned the family down.

Thankfully there are only a few days left before this vacation is over. I avoid Mrs. M's eyes but I think she knows. I think she can smell the sex on us both when we come into the cabin. The joy is gone. I just want it to be over. Mr. M suggests more driving lessons, but I make the excuse that I just want to spend as much time with the girls as possible since I will be going back to boarding school soon.

30

Take This Job and Shove It

Once we get back to the house, I pack up my shit and wait for Monday to come. The girls and I make one last trip to A&W so I can give them all the treats they want. I ask them "what was your favorite thing this summer?"

Judy quickly replies, "You!"

All the girls laugh and agree. I don't ask anything more for fear of breaking down in sobs. I can't eat, but I take in every moment knowing each second is a precious gem I will always cherish. Being with them at this moment is the heartbreaking gift of unconditional love.

Back at the house, I tell Mrs. M I will be back in an hour and I ask Miss Sarah for a ride home. I leave Blue Blaze for Judy.

When I get home, I call Mrs. M and apologize but "my father wants me to be home to spend time with him before going back to school." She says she understands. I hope not, but I think she does.

I rarely leave my Elvis sanctuary. I hate myself and I hate Mr. M.

In my doom and gloom there comes a ray of light. Jeff calls and says there is a letter for me at the office from a Martina Fox. I tell him I will be right over. She says she is leaving right after Labor Day for Chicago, so if I can come to school early, we could spend some time together before she goes. I make my train reservations immediately and I write to Martina that I will be there.

I don't need any new clothes now that I have lost weight, so I spend some money buying presents for my "Sisters" for Christmas. I try to think of something special to buy Martina, but what do you get for the girl who has everything?

My depression is still with me but once again I know that I am resilient. I have survived neglect and wounds that will scar over but never heal. I will just bury it all deep and move on. No sense in building a shrine to it.

31
Junior Year 1959-60

Martina was waiting for me when I got off the train. Her presence feels like a cozy blanket that warms my cold heart. She seems older even though it's only been about four months. She still looks beautiful with little or no makeup. Her dark hair is shorter now.

"You cut your hair. I like it. It looks like Elizabeth Taylor's hair in *A Place In The Sun.*"

"Well, your ponytail makes me miss my long hair, but this is easier, and nowadays, I'm looking for easier. Where should we go? Are you hungry? Or did you give up eating? You look great by the way."

"I'm hungry and thank you. How about Steak N Shake?"

We eat in the car. The carhop recognizes Martina and asks for her autograph.

"Does that happen a lot?" I ask.

"Uh, I'm a big fish in a little pond. When I get to Chicago, I'll be a little fish in a big pond and no, it doesn't happen a lot."

"Speaking of that, are you over the moon about Chicago?"

"More like overwhelmed. I am so glad that I have Jerry to hold my hand through it all. I mean this is really over my head. I think the radio gig will be kind of like it is here, but we are going to be on during drive time, so we have to step it up a lot.

Plus, we will be rehearsing for a play that will open in December. It's all happening so fast."

"How is married life? Is it fun?"

"It has its moments, but it is not as simple as you might think, or as I thought. Living with another person takes patience and a lot of compromises, and sometimes I feel like I'm the only one doing the work. But then again, how can I complain? I'm blessed. What about you? Tell me about your summer."

"Oh, there isn't much to tell. I was a Mother's helper to a family with three girls. The girls were fun, and I loved that part, but what I thought was a perfect family turned out to have a lot of secrets. I'm sort of disillusioned about families. I mean you and I didn't have a good experience with family, and I thought we were the exception, but we might be the rule. Anyway, that young girl who was full of piss and vinegar and thought she could conquer the world got lost along the way. Now I think I am just full of shit. I don't know anything, and what I do know, I wish I didn't."

"Families! Geez, don't get me started. You know, families, like people, are only as sick as their secrets. You know what, Lolo? You are my family and I am yours. Will you be my sister?"

We leave it that way and promise to write and always be in each other's lives. I want to tell her about the rape, or whatever it was, but shame is my secret. I will pour pink paint on it and forget it ever happened. I am aware that I keep remembering, and then I force myself to forget in hopes that I will forget to remember soon.

She drives me to school and comes in with me to say hello to Sister Joseph. We walk to our old room and she touches her radio and looks around, then out the window. "We had some good times here, Lolo. I'll never forget. Things sure were simple then and we didn't even know it. Learn from last year and just enjoy this year before it's over all too soon."

We hug goodbye and I cannot let go. I want to say, "please hold me before I slip away," but she releases me and she says, "Get that girl back. I need her. The world needs her."

The world needs me? What does that mean? Nobody needs me. I have no use, no purpose.

31

What's a Nice Catholic Girl to Do?

I am glad to be here. I feel safe. I know the routine and how to go along to get along. In a way, this feels more like home than back home ever did.

By the time all the other boarders have arrived, I am all settled in. I have time to check everyone out and evaluate who might want to hang out with me. For sure it isn't Karen, who is giving me the stink eye even though I greeted her like an old pal. Apparently, the train incident has been eating at her all summer.

I'm a floater. A loner. My only friend is Janette in study hall and sometimes we eat lunch together. She loans me a book about Prince Siddhartha who left his palace and riches behind in search of enlightenment. She says to keep it under wraps. I ask her why? She says it's probably verboten and the Sister's won't like it. I ask if it's a dirty novel and she looks at me like I'm an idiot. "Don't you know who the Buddha is?"

"Never heard of him. Sorry. What was he in?"

"Oh, bother! Well, read it and we can talk later, but Buddha means 'The Enlightened One' – like Jesus, only earlier."

I read it, and it's interesting and I think Martina might like it or understand it. I'll try to remember to ask her about it.

The first semester passes in a blur. I spend a quiet Christmas with my Sisters, and I love most of the rituals, but I have a love-hate relationship with Mass. I love the comfort that I feel in the glow of the candles in the chapel. I enjoy the smell of incense, the feel of the holy water on my forehead, and the sounds of the nun's rosary beads. The rhythm of the Latin is like a mesmerizing chant. But there is the resentment I feel when I see Father McDonough getting ready to place the communion wafer on my tongue. The thought of his touch near my mouth sends a shiver through my body. His mere presence brings back the sounds of little voices squealing with joy, "Daddy's home."

One afternoon while cooking with Sister Diane, I tell her that a girl I know was raped last summer by an older man and she is having a hard time forgiving him. "What do you think I should tell my friend to help her?"

I was not expecting the advice I got. "What was your friend wearing that caused this man to sin?" she asks.

"What difference does that make?" I try to keep my voice from shaking.

"Men are easily tempted and provocative clothing, makeup, language, and actions, whether intentional or not, are seen by men as invitations to release their carnal urges. Tell your friend to pray for her forgiveness."

"Doesn't the man have any blame in this situation? Are you saying it's all her fault?"

"Of course, he has responsibility for his own soul, but we are talking about your friend, not him. Look, it's like if you leave a fifty-dollar bill lying around and somebody steals it. The money should have been put away so there wouldn't be any temptation. So, both parties are at fault, not just the thief. In fact, the person who created the temptation may have the bigger culpability."

This conversation ruins the festivities for me. There is no joy. There is no peace. I wish my mind could accept and let go.

I miss Martina. I did get a Christmas card from her and she told me about how she is struggling with all the new changes in her life. She says she is not complaining and is grateful for everything. She included several newspaper articles about her and Jerry and a good review of her performance. She signed it with love and "miss you, Dear Friend."

I wrote back but I have no idea what I wrote. Did I ask her if she knew who Buddha was?

Einstein says there is no time and that is how I feel. No time and no-thing. When I look outside, the grounds are beautiful and peaceful. When I look inside myself, it is dark and ugly and it is hard – no, impossible – to find peace.

Janette tells me all is an illusion. "There is only NOW." That's what Einstein says, and I don't understand either one. Time and space feel weird to me though, and big chunks of time seem to vanish and then I'm back in my body. I have to concentrate to keep it all together. Well, I certainly don't tell anyone.

Easter is here in a flash. What happened in February and March? An Easter card arrives from Miss Sarah. She writes a short note about the resurrection of Jesus, and we are forgiven and we must forgive. Enclosed is a newspaper clipping. Headline: Bank Executive Arrested for Multiple Rapes. There is a picture of Mr. M. They are calling him the Romeo Rapist. Five women identify him and describe his demeanor after the heinous act as if they were complicit lovers. Police records indicate that he had been detained several times for window peeping, but was never charged due to his position in the community and various innocent excuses for his behavior.

I search to find Sister Diane to show her the evidence and hopefully she will see that she misjudged the whole thing. When I find her, I am in a frenzy to explain that this is the man I told her about. "Read it. Read it. He is the guilty one. Read it."

She says "I'm glad that he has been arrested. What else do you want me to say? Forgive him."

That is just fucked up and I tell her so.

I feel like I am in another time. The energy and vibration I feel in my body have slowed down; the ground beneath my feet is unstable. The silence implodes in my head. The walls of my room are thinking and feeling the things that I cannot, and yet it is all me. I am nothing. I am everything.

"Wake up. Wake up."

32

Summer of 1960

"Wake up, Loretta. Do you hear me? Wake up"

"Okay, okay, I'm awake. Why do I have to wake up?" This seems like a logical question. I'm annoyed because I was having a wonderful dream. Good dreams are hard to come by and should never be interrupted.

"Do you know where you are?"

"Of course. Why wouldn't I know where I am?"

"Then tell me where you are?"

"Why? Don't you know?"

"Okay, let's change the question. Do you know who I am?"

"Oh, I know this one. You are the annoying bitch who is waking me up from a good dream to ask me stupid questions. Now leave me alone so I can go back to sleep."

"How old are you, Loretta?"

"Oh my god, you are just not going to let this go, are you?"

"Not until you answer one of these questions. It's your choice?"

"You answer mine first. Why do I have to get up?"

"You have to get up because it's time to get up and start your day. There is a schedule here. If you want breakfast, you better get up?"

"I don't like you."

"I know. Go take a shower."

I don't want to admit that I don't know where I am, and I don't know how old I am or who that bitch is that is so interested in giving me the third degree. I give in and go to the room she is pointing at and take a shower. The warm water feels good and wakes me up, but it does nothing to help me with answers.

Now that I'm in the shower, I don't want to leave the shower. It seems like too much work to get out. I'll just stay in here until something else happens. I don't feel afraid. Something about all this feels familiar, but for the life of me, I don't know why. Why can't I remember?

Oh right. Silly me I must have been dreaming so hard I forgot I'm at school. That lady must be new. I hurry and get dressed in the clothes that are laid out for me. It's just a smock so I assume Sister Diane wants me to wear it to work for some reason. When I go out into my bedroom, that lady is still there.

"I'll walk with you to breakfast if that's okay with you, Loretta?"

"Yeah, sure. I'm sorry I just don't remember who you are. I don't have a very good memory today. Are you new here?" She takes my arm and we head out the door and into a hallway. "Hey, I've never been in this wing of the school before."

"Let's walk this way. You and I have met before and I'm not new. You are. We can talk more about how we met over breakfast. Are you hungry?"

"No, not really. I could go for some chocolate milk or a Popsicle would be nice."

We enter a small dining room that is empty except for us and a lady who brings our breakfast. I guess there are no choices. Oatmeal, it is. Nice and lumpy so it requires lots of sugar and milk. The lady just has coffee. She loads it up with plenty of sugar and milk. Maybe we have things in common. I'll be patient.

"What is the last thing you remember?"

"Ah, I remember you putting too much sugar in your coffee." I think I have just pulled a fast one on her, but she ignores me.

"Do you want me to tell you where you are, why you are here, and what we need to work on while you are here?"

"Wow, I'm really glad you said that because I am not going to pass this test without your help."

"My name is Dr. Sharon Westphall, and you are at Pleasant Valley Sanitarium. Stop me if you recall any of this."

"Am I sick?"

"Not in a physical way, but yes, in a mental way. You had a psychotic break with reality, which is usually brought on by a traumatic event. Like what soldiers go through after war sometimes. They call that shell shock, caused by the trauma of seeing or physically experiencing something so horrific that the mind doesn't want to accept it. We have not discovered what might have happened to you to cause this break, and that is what we – you and I – are here to work on. Does any of this make sense to you?"

"Is this a nut house? Am I crazy? Can I leave if I feel like this is a big mistake?"

"This is not a "nut house" and I think you have already made a lot of progress whether you realize it or not. Your Father will sign you out when you are well."

"This is worse than I thought."

"Why do you say that?"

"I don't know. I just feel unsafe right now."

"You are safe. I promise no one will hurt you. We are here to help you get well. When you first came here four months ago, you thought you were four years old. You were talking like a very small child. You couldn't pronounce your name Loretta; instead, you said Lolo. You told me you killed your Mother and that nobody loved you, you didn't have any friends and you were not very smart. What do you think of that?"

"Sounds about right, I guess. I mean, I hope I'm not in here for murder, but so far, I would say I must be pretty dumb. Do highly intelligent people end up here?"

"This has nothing to do with IQ. Everything you told me that you must have thought about yourself at four is totally not true. You have lots of people who love you, and you are very smart."

"Oh yeah, prove it."

"You came here from Sacred Heart Academy where you were on the Honor Roll for two years. The Nuns apparently love you very much and that is why you are here so they can visit you and continue to care for you instead of sending you back to your hometown where your Father says he would not have the time to devote to your recovery like Sister Joseph and the other Sister's would. Regardless, they could have shipped you off as not their responsibility, but they are here for you. Also, there is a schoolmate, Janette, who considers you a great friend. She comes every Saturday to visit with you. Every Saturday for months! Martina Fox, also a friend, has called and sent many cards. There are letters from Sarah Johnson. So, you see you are loved, you do have friends and you are smart."

"I do remember going to Sacred Heart for a year with Martina. She is a good friend and helped me understand algebra and that's why I was on the Honor Roll. The second year is not clear in my memory."

"If you are finished with your breakfast, I would like to get you into an activity that will be relaxing for you. What do you enjoy doing that lets you express your creativity?"

"I like to color. I like to play jacks, but I guess I'm too old for that. Hey, sounds like you are reading my mail so stop that."

"I am not reading your mail. I just noticed who it was from, and I have talked to Martina when she has called. How about we get you set up with some art supplies so you can spend some time creating until our next session? Or would you like to talk some more?"

"I would like to color for a while. Can I go back to my room?" I needed time to make sense of what she has just told me.

33

The Truth Will Set You Free

When I get to my room, I take my first conscious look around. It is a basic sterile cube with no indication of anyone residing here, except for a desk and chair and an unmade bed. I immediately make the bed from habit. A messy bed is a messy mind. Maybe I should have left it alone.

I poke my head out the door and I hear muffled voices and weird noises through the vents. Who knows what is going on in this place? I assess the bare gray walls of my room with three small rectangle windows too high to look out. I wonder if I can get Martina's radio. The room smells like some kind of cleaning chemicals, maybe something that would kill bugs. What could I get that would make it smell better? I can't think of anything except baking food, like biscuits. No, not biscuits. Chocolate cake baking in the oven, or apple pie.

I can almost smell it when Dr. Sharon interrupts. Her voice makes me jump. I never heard her coming. I wonder if she surprised me on purpose. I don't trust her.

"Here's a box of art supplies. If you need something that isn't in here, just let me know. I'll be back in a couple of hours. Have you thought about anything that we talked about earlier?"

"I think the smell of this room is disturbing. Do you smell it?" She sniffs the air like a raccoon. She kind of looks like a raccoon. Unruly looking gray, brown, blackish hair. Dark circles under her eyes and a pinched face with frown lines across her forehead.

"It smells like disinfectant. Does it bother your breathing?" She is full of questions.

"Yes, it makes me not want to breathe. Can you ask them to just use soap and water?"

"I'll work on it. I'll be back to take you to lunch."

"Ooh, I can't wait." I wonder if she gets sarcasm.

I don't feel like drawing or doing anything except crawling back in bed, but then again, maybe I should make some art for my walls. Wall art! Wall art! I know what I'll do. I'll decorate with Elvis pictures. Yeah! Something to look forward to. Meanwhile, I'll indulge Dr. Sharon and draw something.

"Are you ready for lunch?"

"Goddamn it, stop sneaking up on me! You need to put a bell around your neck or whistle *Dixie* before you come in. And no, I'm not hungry. That lumpy oatmeal is sitting like a brick in my stomach, but you go ahead." Please!

"That's fine. I can wait. Can I see what you drew?"

"Knock yourself out." I hand her the only one I did.

"Let's see if I understand what I'm looking at? There are three little girls, one bigger girl, a bicycle, a cake, and all of the girls are crying big tears, except for the girl in the sky. Do you know who these girls are?"

"No. Well, yes. I'm not sure."

"Why are all these girls crying?"

"I don't know. I guess they are sad."

"Why did you only use the color black for your picture?"

"Put this on your list of things to work on. Find me magazines with pictures of Elvis. I don't know why I only used black. Maybe because I felt like it and black is beautiful. Nuns wear black. You must like it too. Do you always wear black skirts?" I think I've just turned the tables on her.

"You got me there. I do wear a lot of blacks. Would you like to be a nun?"

"Fuck no! No fucking way. That's a joke – get it?"

"What do you know about fucking, Loretta?"

"I'm really uncomfortable talking about this. I suggest you ask someone else or read a book. I would think at your age you would tell me. I do think I am hungry now, and I would like to have lunch and then take a nap. I don't mean 'imagine time.' I mean a real nap."

"What does 'imagine time' mean?"

"Fuck if I know." I think this may be my go-to answer to all her stupid questions.

A flood of people and questions pour in like the dam just broke and I'm right in its path. It's sink or swim and I'm paddling my ass off with no life preserver in sight.

Dr. Sharon has called in recruits. They are all men with beards and glasses and shiny chrome domes. They ask me questions about my mother and my father, and do I have any other relatives?

"Fuck if I know." It's my answer and it's the truth but they think I'm hiding something.

I ask them, "Are all Psychiatrists bald and nearsighted? Is that beard hiding something? Did you go into this profession to cure yourself?"

Eventually, they do not return, and Dr. Sharon is stuck with me. Sister Joseph came and brought me my textbooks. She says there is a tutor for me if I feel like I want to continue with my studies while I'm here. I'm looking forward to doing something besides making pictures for Dr. Sharon to analyze. My walls are covered with drawings and a few pictures of Elvis. I think he is in Germany. There are not as many pictures to be had, but thanks to Janette, I have a few really good ones.

When Janette comes, we get to go outside and sit in the sun. I am grateful for her friendship. We talk about music and how shitty it has become since Elvis left and Buddy Holly died in a plane crash. There are still some good ones like The Everly Brothers and Dion, but then there are the "Teen Idols" created in hopes of replacing Elvis. Bobby Rydell, Frankie Avalon, Tommy Sands, Fabian. "Oh please. Let me up." Janette laughs at my sarcasm.

I do like Ricky Nelson. I always have since I was a kid; maybe more because we have the same last name, but he's no Elvis. The worst is Pat Boone, the answer to a mother's wet dream.

Still, I am thankful to have my radio in my room. The TV room on my floor is small. Only a couple of women come in and they argue over what program to watch. Loud voices make me feel like something dangerous could happen, so I only go when no one else is there.

Janette and I talk a lot about religion, too. She says she is a "seeker" in search of the truth. She is skeptical of what she calls the Jesus myth. She says "I do love me some Jesus, but the whole virgin birth and dying for our sins doesn't make sense. What did we do that was so horrible? Eat an apple? So now God has to send his son to suffer and die? Why couldn't he just say 'Okay, you screwed up, but I forgive you?' The end."

"Yeah, it does make God seem like kind of a dick." I think we don't really know anything about Jesus or God, but I like to hear her talk, so I just agree.

I'm pretty sure Dr. Sharon doesn't know what she is doing. There doesn't seem to be any progress or maybe we've made all the progress we need to make, and I should just go back to regular school. I don't know what she wants from me. She told me I'm lucky that I came back into my own body instead of continuing to think I was four years old. She says most people don't recover. So, I say "Thanks for doing that and are we finished here?"

"Not until we find out what happened in the first place so we can work on healing that trauma." She insists.

By the 4th of July, we have not made any headway. I tell her "I think it might be because I have had a lot of losses in my life: my mother, Miss Sarah, Mrs. Boxer, Margaret, and Sandy. It seems like everyone I care about leaves me. Isn't that enough?"

"I think that is a major source, but what happened last April that pushed you over the edge?"

"Have you talked to Sister Joseph? Does she know anything?"

"She said you should tell me about Oona. Janette says sometimes you said you were Oona. She thought it was a game that you were playing, like being an actress. She said you were very good at it. Your whole demeanor would change."

"I don't know anything about this Oona." I don't tell her, but it does sound familiar. What is it? Who is she?

34

But First it will Piss You Off

I'm invited to dinner with my Sisters. It is just like old home week except I feel depressed. I help Sister Diane make pies while I think about suicide, but how?

Now, Sister tells me that we will be having dinner with jackass Father McDonough.

"I'm not feeling very well, Sister. I would like to go back. Can someone pick me up?"

"I'm sorry, dear. Are you going to be all right alone there?" Sister Diane is concerned and I don't want to worry her.

"I'll be fine. Don't worry. I don't want to spoil your dinner by worrying about me. I'll be fine. I'm just really tired."

"Should I have Father McDonough take you back?"

"NO!" Easy girl, calm down. "I mean no. I can take a cab or something."

"He won't mind, I'm sure. I'll ask him."

NO! No, no, no." I'm scaring Sister. I can see the confusion on her face. Her sweet, chubby, red-baked face.

"I'm going to call a cab. I, I, I, have to go."

"All right. Don't get upset, Loretta. I will call. You just fix yourself a plate to go and some cookies, too. I'll be right back."

Okay. I'm Okay. My throat is dry. I have no saliva to swallow. My head is throbbing, my heart is pounding and I'm sweating profusely. I might be having a heart attack. No, I'm too young for that. It's just . . . fuck if I know. I'll sit down and put my head between my legs. I think I saw that in a movie. Breathe deeply and slowly. Easy does it. I'm okay.

"Loretta?" Sister Joseph is here. Oh shit.

"Hi, Sister." I jump to my feet and look for food to pack up. "So many choices of good things to take with me. It's hard to choose." I laugh nervously.

"Sister Diane says she thinks you are not feeling well and maybe you should stay the night."

"No, no. I'm just tired and I want my own bed, but thank you, Sister, for everything. Can you get me a cab?"

"I'll drive you, honey, if you are sure that's what you want."

"Yes, Sister, thank you. Thank you."

In the car on the way, Sister says, "Sister Diane said you became quite agitated when she suggested Father McDonough could drive you home. Did Father do something to you?"

"Oh, gosh, no. I'm sorry if I gave that impression. I just didn't want to put anyone out on my account, especially today."

I change the subject to small talk about my tutor and how I'm looking forward to coming back to school in September. I jump out of the car before it comes to a complete stop, and almost drop my bag of food.

"Thanks again, Sister." Inside, I close my eyes and breathe a sigh of relief. Maybe I will never leave this place.

On Saturday I ask Janette to tell me about Oona.

She says "I don't know what to say. I mean, you would just be her sometimes. I never knew who was going to show up, but I could tell immediately just by the posture. She walked differently than you. Here's how I think you two were different. She was very much in control and a tough cookie. You like to act like you are a tough cookie, but there is something very vulnerable about you – an insecurity that Oona doesn't possess. She is smart and knows it. You are smart but you don't seem to know it. I like you both. Do you know why you put on that act?"

"I didn't even know I was putting on an act. I don't remember anything about Oona. And where did that name come from? I mean, what's an Oona?" We both laugh, but it's not funny.

Janette gave me two books. One to keep and the other was a loaner on numerology. I love this book. I think Einstein said the whole universe is numbers, or maybe I just said that. The premise is that all things are in cycles, like the seasons, or day and night, and there are cycles in years starting with a one year and ending in a nine-year. Then it starts back with a one year and we begin the cycle all over again. Whatever falls shall rise again, and whatever rises shall fall again. Funny how so many things can come back to the Bible or other philosophies.

Ecclesiastes 3:1 To everything there is a season and a time for every purpose under heaven.

Patience is power; with time and patience, the mulberry leaf becomes silk. This is a Chinese proverb.

To know what the cycle I am in, I add the numbers of this year and then reduce to one digit. $1+9+5+9 = 24 = 2+4 = 6$

I am surprised that this is a six-year and wonder how it makes sense for me. The book says a six-year is about "Vision and Acceptance. It is a time to accept and to appreciate the bigger picture of what has been, what is to become, and what lies beyond."

Next year will be a seven year. That is about Trust and Openness. "It will be a time for enjoyment and ease; a time to look back and learn from the years that have come before."

When I go to the TV room to watch Ozzie and Harriet so I

can see Ricky Nelson sing, the two women are there. I think about Vision and Acceptance and I wonder how I can work this to my advantage. I am ready to accept whatever happens.

"Hello, ladies. It's funny that we haven't met before since I think we are the only ones on this floor. My name is Loretta and it's nice to meet you." They look at me but look back at the TV.

"It gets kind of boring around here sometimes, and I wonder if you like to play cards?"

"Sshhh. We are trying to watch TV."

"Okay, enjoy your program." I get that two's company and three's a crowd. At least they agree on that. I think the next time I go to the TV room and they are there, I will just watch whatever is on and shut my mouth. I'll leave it up to them to make a move.

Dr. Sharon comes back the following Monday. It's good to see someone who will talk about anything.

I asked her what she did on vacation. She said "I attended a seminar in Canada on a new drug called LSD. Dr. Osmond said he has had a lot of success with his patients ending serious addictions to alcohol and patients that normally would be treated with electric shock treatments. The drug causes hallucinations where the patient experiences God or the oneness with everything and a certain understanding that changes the patient in astounding ways."

"Wow, did you bring any back with you?"

"No, but I am going to keep in contact with him and follow his progress. What did you do?"

"Not much. I started studying a book on numerology that is pretty interesting. I went to Siena Hall for a visit. We had a nice visit, but I just wasn't into it. That's it."

"That's it? Nothing else?" She persists.

"Oh, yeah, I tried to get the two ladies in the TV room to talk to me. They joined forces and shut me up, but I don't call that anything like news."

"Sister Joseph said you got pretty upset about having Father McDonough bring you back here. She thinks there is more to it. Do you want to talk about it?"

"I'm not sure what that was all about. Maybe I just don't like him and how he pushes his way in and gets treated like we should all bow down. Plus, I don't like that Priests are the only ones who can do the Mass or serve communion. They get all the glory and the nuns do all the work. I don't like it and I don't want to be around him, especially alone in a car."

"Why especially in a car? Did something happen to you in a car?"

"I don't like cars. I never really thought about it, but now that you mention it, I was in the back seat of a car watching Miss Sarah disappear from my life, and I was watching Sandy in the back seat of her father's car when she left me, so maybe that's it. Cars ruin everything. They take things away from me."

"But you were okay with Sister driving you, yes?"

"Well, the common denominator here seems to be that I don't like men in cars."

"You seem to be getting angry now. Is that how you feel?"

"Yes, I'm feeling angry. Mostly at myself because I should be letting this go. I heard 'what you resist, persists' and I'm trying to let it go and I don't know why it's so hard. But I think I just need time and it will work itself out."

"Tell me about Oona. Is she here?"

"No, no she's not here. You don't see her, do ya?"

"I think she is here, and you could tell her to show up."

"No, she is not here, and I don't talk to her. How could I if she isn't here?"

"Does she know why you don't like men in cars?"

"This conversation is too weird, and now I have a headache. I'll see you tomorrow."

"Could you call Oona and ask her to come, just for one time?"

"Sure, I'll ask her, whatever."

35
Letting Go

Today is a wonderful day. I have two letters to read. One is from Martina and the other one is from Miss Sarah. I read Martina's first. She is doing great, had a wonderful vacation in Italy. She is trying to make more time to call so we can talk but just manages to write on her way to somewhere. I rip open Miss Sarah's letter. There is a newspaper clipping; Romeo Rapist Sentenced to 20 Years. It's him. The car, the man, the loss, and the guilt.

"Loretta? What's wrong? Talk to me. Get it out so you can let it go." Dr. Sharon is standing over me. I'm in the fetal position on my bed and I can't stop the pain. The pain in my heart is so deep I can hardly breathe. She sees the letter and the newspaper clipping on the floor and reads the headline. "Did he rape you? Is this the man in the car?"

"Help me," I gasp.

"Tell Oona to talk to me, Loretta. I know she is here. Let her tell me so I can help you."

Silence, and then Oona sits up and speaks,

"Hello, Dr. Sharon. I'm here to help. Loretta is relieved that I can tell you what she cannot." She points to the clipping. "He is the man in the car. He is the father of the girls Loretta took care of last summer. She ruined the family. She is guilty. He told her so and so did Sister Diane. It's all her fault. Can you help her or will this pain in her heart kill her? I'm very fearful for her."

Dr. Sharon and Oona talk for a long time. Oona tells her what happened in embarrassing detail. When she is finished, Dr. Sharon thanks her and asks if Loretta can now speak for herself?

Oona says, "Loretta can now talk about it also. The truth has set her free and that frees me to leave, but I will always have her back."

Over the next few weeks, Dr. Sharon explains about our shadow side. That is the part of us that we don't want to admit belongs to us, so we project it on others. Mr. M couldn't face the truth that he was a rapist, so he had to believe that the women were complicit; they wanted it and he was just doing what they wanted. He couldn't control his carnal urges, his need to control another, to dominate. It wasn't about sex. It was about power over another person. He was cruel and selfish.

"Sister says I need to forgive myself and him. What do you think about that?"

"Well, ever since the story of Adam and Eve, it has always been a woman to blame. Poor hapless Adam had no power to resist Eve and her seductive apple. Since all religions are patriarchal, it's very convenient to cast the woman as the downfall of man.

I think Sister Diane is right, but probably not for the reasons she thinks. Sister Diane may have become a nun before she had any real experience in the world, so all she knows about men and sex are what she gets from the men of the church, so her opinions are based solely on the teachings that women are the temptresses.

Yes, you need to forgive yourself. Not for being a sinner, but for being human – for being young and not knowing how to keep yourself safe – but you are not to blame. You are not guilty and feeling guilty is a waste of energy. It serves no good purpose. It's always hardest to forgive ourselves, and I think that is the best part of confession because sometimes we just need someone else to say, "You are forgiven." You are a good person, Loretta. You didn't deserve what he did and you are not responsible for his actions. It's all on him."

"But I looked – and I peeked to see him naked. I am guilty. That is what caused it."

"You are still a child and children are curious. Especially about the body. Forgive yourself for being curious, for being human, and I think you have to forgive Mr. M because he is selfish and there is no cure for it. Forgive him so you can be healed. But forgiveness doesn't mean it was okay."

Over the next several weeks we talked and talked until I accepted what happened as a part of the suffering of life and chose not to suffer anymore. I didn't tell Dr. Sharon all my shameful secrets, but I accepted those parts of me also. There was no good outcome of telling everything anyway. She and I became close and a real bond formed. We were no longer Dr. and patient, but good friends.

36

Share the Good News

By late July, I no longer needed Oona for support although I know she will always be a part of me – the healing part of me and maybe the coping part of me. I owe her my life. I looked forward to being a senior and back in school in September.

"Good morning, Loretta.

"Good morning Dr. Sharon. What's up?"

Let's go to breakfast together so we can chat."

Over breakfast, she said "I want to be perfectly honest with you. I think you can handle the situation, so I won't whitewash it."

"Wow, this sounds serious. Now what?"

"It's not that bad. In fact, I think we can turn this into a good thing. I spoke to your father and he will release you to go back to school in September, but in the meantime, you are going to stay here. Basically, he doesn't want the responsibility of having you home for the month. I hope you don't take this personally and get your feelings hurt. He's just a man and doesn't really know what to do with a teenage girl. Besides, he is busy with his company, so you understand, right?"

"Oh, I understand. It's you that doesn't understand, but that's okay. What am I supposed to do this month? Stay locked up here?"

"Well, that's why I think we can make this into a good thing. You can be free, within reason, to come and go as you please. This is essentially a pretty expensive hotel he's willing to pay for, and I have no qualms about adding my services to his bill and giving you a substantial allowance so you can shop and go to movies and enjoy restaurants with Janette or even me. How does that sound?"

"It sounds fuckin' fantastic! Does it start right now?"

"Um, sure. What would you like to do?"

"Everything you mentioned. Show me around town. I have never seen much of it, and in the Fall, I will be a Senior with privileges, so it would be good to already know what to do and where to go. Is there a movie we could catch and then a nice dinner? My treat."

We both laugh. Take that old man.

She suggests that I take a short summer class to get me back in the habit of studying. I ask her to see if there are any extra-curricular classes that I can take on interior design or drafting classes at the Community College?

It turns out I can take both. One is on Tuesdays and one on Thursdays. I'm using the kitchen at home as a model, or I should say remodel. It's actually fun and still gives me time to go out with Janette and shop and to movies with Sharon.

Janette and I spend our days at the community pool. She is going steady with Larry, a guy she met last year at a football game, so most nights she is with him, but sometimes he invites me along. I'm sure Janette makes him though. Larry will be going to college in the fall and we both think that makes him a real catch. We mostly go play miniature golf or just ride around. He says he can fix me up with one of his friends, but I am happy being the third wheel or staying on my own.

On Saturday nights, we end up at Janette's house watching

the cheesy horror movies on late night TV and making wise-cracks. Janette's mom, Annie, makes popcorn for us and I usually stay all night. I like Annie's sense of fun. As a single mother, she is more like a girlfriend to us both. She has her own business as a beautician in her home, and she lets us use her equipment and supplies. Janette likes to change the color of her hair to different shades of blonde and red. I am not that brave, plus I like my black hair. It might be my best feature.

The three of us have in-depth conversations about different religions and philosophies. Annie is well read and quotes Mary Baker Eddy, Edgar Cayce, Norman Vincent Peale, Charles Fillmore, Plato, and Ernest Holmes.

She is a big fan of the Ouija board and we have many fun sessions. She puts both her hands on the device, and she claims it is moving on its own. I have doubts, but when I do it with her, I know I'm not pushing it, and I can feel that she is not either, so I guess I believe.

We ask it questions like will I get married and how many kids will I have? Ouija tells me that yes, I will get married, but when I ask "when," it goes to 20 and it will not say if it is in 20 years or when I'm 20 or 20 months. I ask again "when?" It spells out "love yourself." It says I will have five children, so I think it is full of shit.

When we ask about Janette, it says she will marry Larry. When? 6. Six what? It insists 6 months, but we think this can't be right. It predicts two children, but it doesn't know when. Annie won't even ask if she will get married. I think she doesn't want a husband because she could have her pick if she wanted one.

She has gotten us into politics also. It's an easy transition because John Kennedy is dreamy, and his wife is beautiful. Politics and religion, the two subjects never to be discussed in polite company are, of course, the most satisfying mysteries to ponder. Everything feels right with the world. I couldn't be happier.

37

Senior Year 1960-61

It's good to be back at Sienna Hall. I feel like I am a better me than I have ever been. Thank you, Dr. Sharon. I'm ready for life again.

The first day back all the boarders are congregated in the cafeteria for orientation. A new girl sat down beside me and we exchange nods as Sister begins the yearly address that I could now recite with her because it hasn't changed in three years. When she concludes, we begin filling out our class schedule.

"Hi, I'm Katherine," the new girl said in a whisper that made me pay close attention.

I smile, "Hi, I'm Loretta." Not sure why I'm whispering also.

She leans in and I can smell garlic on her breath. "Could you help me? I'm not sure what courses I should take, or how to fill out this form."

I put my paperwork down beside the book I've been reading and ask her, "What are your interests?"

"Music. Art. Dancing. Fun." She gives me a disarming broad smile. Her toothy wide mouth takes up the biggest part of her face. Her fragile light blonde hair frames her flawless pale skin. She literally glistens. I learn later the only cosmetic she uses is Vaseline. A dab on her lips and a slight pass over her lashes and brows. It doesn't look greasy. It just makes her pink lips look moist and kissable and gives her light lashes and brows just a little definition.

"So, let's sign you up for music and art and how about typing? Typing is kind of "fun" and it's easy and a skill that could come in handy someday." I'm filling out the form even though she has not agreed to my suggestions.

She looks at the book I have closed and put aside. "Oh, I've read *There Is A River*. I know all about Edgar Cayce." Then she babbles on about something altogether new, while I continue to fill out her form and select classes, even though I have no idea if they are what she wants. It doesn't seem to matter to her as long as the paperwork gets done.

When I hand her the completed forms, she says thanks and takes off. I try to keep an eye on her, but she is like Tinker Bell in the wind. She's here; she's there; she's landed and off again.

I don't have her to myself until later that evening in the leisure room. She is shy now. She approaches me with caution and sits just out of earshot. It forces me to move towards her. She's like a cat that keeps you chasing it and then relents and lets you pet it so that you feel somehow grateful for the favor.

"Are you all settled in?" I ask.

"Sort of. I mean, this is a big place and I've been trying to figure out where everything is, so I haven't had time to put my things away. Are you unpacked?"

"Yes, but this is my third year here so there isn't that much for me to do that I haven't done before. How did you end up here?"

"Well, my parents are missionaries and my older sister is in charge, but she is pretty bossy, and I just don't like her telling me what to do, so she said she wasn't going to be responsible anymore, and here I am."

"Missionaries? Wow, what is that like?"

"That is just another word for two people who should never have had five children because they are children themselves. They like to travel and be free. That's what that is like. They are totally irresponsible, but most people think they're very fun to have around. I wouldn't know."

"Does that make you mad or sad?" I'm curious.

"Neither, really. I want to be just like them, but no kids. My father plays the guitar, mother sings and they both love to dance. They just enjoy life in spite of five kids. Hey, do you want to come to my room?"

When we enter her room, she steps over all the clothes and things strewn around that she has brought with her. She sits on her bed and grabs her guitar and begins to strum a tune.

"Shouldn't you be putting things away?" I ask.

"Would you do it? I mean, since you've done it before you probably know the best way."

The next thing I know, I'm doing all her work while she plays. I didn't even see it coming. I try to engage her in conversation by referring back to the book I was reading, and she gives me little tidbits that keep me coming back.

"What do you think about Karma?" I ask while I fold her clothes and stack them in organized piles.

"Oh, yeah, the best part is that we come back in groups, like family. Cayce says we actually pick our parents. And there is so much karma in families that you can't tell who owes who from a past life. And you can't judge anyone. He says "there is so much good in the worst of us and so much bad in the best of us that you can't judge."

This makes me stop in my tracks. "Bullshit! I would never have picked my father."

She laughs. It starts with a low aahh and then rises in pitch and volume. It's the kind of laugh that is infectious and I laugh with her. When we stop laughing, she continues.

"Edgar Cayce says you don't have to believe it. It's up to you. He isn't trying to convert anyone. All of the information that comes to him in a trance is news to him too. As a Southern Baptist Sunday school teacher, reincarnation, astrology, karma, and chakras are all foreign concepts to him."

I continue to organize the clothes that are scattered around and ask, "Why did you bring so many jeans and tops? Two pairs of jeans would be plenty."

"Back-up!" She says. "They're all different in some way so I have choices. I also have difficulty making decisions – what to leave in and what to leave out. And, finally, I don't want my sister wearing my stuff."

She has a suitcase filled with pictures cut out of magazines or collected from some unknown place. One is of Jesus and his Sacred Heart. Another is a picture of our Milky Way with an arrow that says "You are Here." There are several pictures of beautiful babies and different ethnic children and one of Marilyn Monroe. There are exotic materials and beautiful eclectic figurines and small bowls.

"What do you want to do with this stuff?"

"Oh, it's to make this room beautiful. You can decorate. Can you cover the window with some material? Go ahead, you decide."

By nine o'clock, I have most of her clothes put away and her room looks neat and tidy. I have had more fun decorating, and it makes me wish I had made my room special. She thanks me and flatters me saying, "You have a real talent for organization and decorating. I bet there is a business doing that."

This just seems like common sense to me, but I am feeling a little superior about it now.

"You're welcome. I'll see you in the morning. Sleep tight and don't let the bed bugs bite."

"Are there really bed bugs?" She looks around on her bed in fright.

"No. It's just an expression." I realize I have to watch my words.

"Good. Will you come to get me in the morning so I don't get lost?"

She looks like a little orphan afraid of the dark. I can feel her anxiety.

"Sure. I'll be here bright and early. We go to Mass first and then breakfast. Good night."

38

Katherine

The next morning, I tap on her door. "Good morning, Katherine." No answer. I knock, "Katherine?"

A sleepy voice answers. "What?"

"It's time to go. Are you ready?" I don't wait for an answer. I open the door. Holy Moly, she is still in bed.

"Get up! Hurry." I begin throwing pieces of her uniform at her. "Come on."

She moves at a snail's pace, and I practically have to dress her. We make it to Mass just in time. I'm annoyed, and I think to myself, *I've had enough of this crap. I'm not doing this again.*

She follows me to breakfast. I'm happy that I am not working in the kitchen this year, due to my fragile condition per Dr. Sharon. What a pal. I fill my tray and beat a path to a table where there is only one seat left. I do a lot of nodding and smiling even though I am not part of the conversation, but I need to look like I am.

The bell rings and I head for homeroom. I regret that I have assigned Katherine to my homeroom. The next thing I know, she is walking beside me.

"I was so nervous last night that I couldn't get to sleep. Thanks for getting me up."

I say "Okay," but I'm waiting for an apology that doesn't come. I help her navigate her classes in the morning, but by noon I try to escape to eat lunch with Janette.

I see where Janette is sitting, and I rush to begin a conversation with her, so if Katherine does join the table, at least my back will be to her and maybe she will get the hint. She does join the table but sits at the end facing Janette and must be working that little girl lost face because Janette falls for it.

"Hey, what's with the new girl?" It's a rhetorical question that is followed up with "Hey, new girl. Come and sit by us." I make a soft groan that I hope Janette will pick up on and cool it.

"What did she say?" Janette is asking me. I turn to look at Katherine who is doing the whisper trick, but it's too late to warn Janette. Janette gets up and moves to the end of the table. She is drawn in like a guppy going down a drain. "Move down, Lo."

I can't figure out if Katherine is the dumbest or smartest one at the table. Either way, she now has our full attention. She offers us both a garlic clove and explains, "It is really good for your digestion. Mix it in with your mashed potatoes."

She and Janette carry on a great conversation about their lives and interests. I can't help adding that she has read *There Is a River*, and with that, Janette gets the conversation that I was trying to coerce out of Katherine last night. I am now happy that we ended up together and I am hanging on their every word.

"Thoughts are things," they say in unison and laugh in agreement.

When we leave the lunchroom, I anticipate Katherine will once again want my help, but instead, Janette now takes over.

I feel a little jealous which makes no sense at all. One minute I'm trying to get rid of her and the next minute I want her to be with me. Maybe I always want what I don't have. I self-talk: *Take it easy Loretta. She'll be yours at dinner.* And indeed, she is. I ask her how her first day went?

"Oh, pretty good. I think I'm getting the lay of the land. I like Janette. Lunch was fun. How was your day?"

I hesitate for a few seconds debating if I should bring up this morning or let it go. I need to get it out. "It was a rough start and I didn't like being rushed. I don't like being late and I think you should apologize." There is a long silence and I finally cave and say, "but I also enjoyed lunch with you and Janette."

"I know I can be a lot." She says. "My sister says I am here to teach patience and she says she has learned enough. She said, 'Go teach somewhere else.' Edgar Cayce says, 'Patience is the measure of our understanding'."

Those disclosures have me in the crosshairs of embarrassment and letting go.

She stops abruptly and looks into my eyes. "I will not apologize for being myself, but if I hurt you, then I'm sorry for that."

She interrupts my equanimity by asking if she can come and see my room. I say "of course." By the time we reach my room. I have a new perspective. Just 24 hours ago I was feeling very smug about my pristine room and my rigid rules. Now, I am embarrassed about my lack of creativity and flexibility. We both look around my room. I see it with new eyes.

"Wait here. I'll be back in a minute. Which way is my room?" she asks.

39
All You Need is Love

When she returns, she has her suitcase of many pleasures. "Here. Create." She curls up on my bed and watches me as I transform my room into a sanctuary of colors and mystical dreamscapes. I put a piece of red material over the lampshade and it softens the dream.

When I am finished, I lie beside her and take it all in. I love the smell of garlic escaping from her pores and the earthy smell of her underarms because she doesn't believe in deodorant or shaving. She cuddles into me and I listen to her breathing. It seems like a miracle of two bodies and two minds merging into one consciousness. It seems to be the most natural communion without a plan. I am in love.

The next day we are inseparable. I cannot wipe the smile off my face, nor do I want to. I float from class to class and search the halls for a glimpse of her face. At lunch, Janette says, "You two look like the cats that swallowed the canary. What's up?"

Katherine giggles. I say, "Just happy to be with good friends. We only have a few months before we are free. Free to be and do whatever we want."

Janette interrupts, "What do you want to do after graduation, Katherine?"

Katherine replies without hesitation, "I think we should put a girl's singing group together and go to New York or California or Philly. Girl groups are just as popular as guys now. What do you think?"

"Katherine, I don't know how to sing or play the guitar or anything. How can we possibly do this?" I am looking for her to give me the magic solution because I would follow her anywhere.

"Everybody can sing. It just takes practice. And all you need to know is a few chords to play the guitar. Let's pick some songs and practice. Are you in, Janette?"

"You might change your mind when you hear me try to carry a tune, but sure, let's do it. I have some 45's at home. We could practice this weekend instead of going downtown."

We have a plan. Delusional, improbable, and implausible, but a joyful plan.

Janette picks us up and we converge on Annie. Annie actually encourages us to try this. "Now is the time to try whatever your heart tells you. There will never be a better time than now."

We invite her to join us for the lesson that Katherine is about to give.

Katherine instructs us to all lie on the floor next to each other. The shades are pulled down and it is relatively dark. That provides a feeling of anonymity.

"Place your hands on your stomach. Singing is all about the breath." We begin by filling our lungs and just making a long noise releasing the air.

"Again, louder, longer." Individually she makes each of us sing the scales. "Louder!"

Janette discovers she has a strong vibrato when she lets go. After a half hour of these exercises, we are no longer shy voices in the dark. We are loud, strong and feeling euphoric. It's probably due to all that oxygen hitting our brains.

"Okay, let's sing a song together." She starts with a song we all know, *Silent Night.* Then someone started *Jingle Bells* and we rotate starting songs until we run out of Christmas themes.

Annie starts one that is popular now: *He's got the whole world in his hands.* By the second line, we all join in. Then Annie starts the next verse, but she changes the words. Now we are all on board making our own song.

Janette starts "We got a whole lot of singing in our life. We got a whole lot of singing in our life." We all pick up the verse, "We got a whole lot of singing in our life".

"Katherine, you go."

"I got a whole lot of lovin in my life. I got a whole lot of lovin' in my life.

"Lo, take it."

"I got a whole lot of nuns in my life. I got a whole lot of nuns in my life. I got a whole lot of nuns in my life."

We all crack up singing this, and then it goes to shoes, boyfriends, dancing, money, peace, joy, Elvis, chocolate, cars, gratitude, friendship and hamburgers.

We now feel hungry, so we stop singing, but we do not get up right away. We stay in the vibration and thank Katherine for a wonderful gift. We found our voices.

40
Girl's Group

There is so much to think about. Life is changing at warp speed. We are all interested in the election. John Kennedy is the handsome Prince and Jackie is the beautiful Princess. It is a fairy tale we can all believe in – especially for Catholics, but I contend, anyone with a television.

Annie teaches us about backcombing our hair to make a bouffant like Jackie's. I have so much thick black hair that when it is all ratted up my head looks enormous. I like it.

We split our time between rehearsing our songs, going to movies, doing our hair and makeup and squeezing in a little studying. Mostly I am in charge of doing homework, and they copy. I don't mind. It's all for one and one for all. We still don't have a name for our group, but we know we will have a blonde and redhead and a brunette.

November 6, 1960, John F. Kennedy is elected President. We are over the moon. The '60s are all about youth and vigor and infinite possibilities. We feel invincible. I am just happy to have a plan that takes me away from Rockton.

I had no idea what to do after high school. I never thought of myself as a scholarly person and I don't really enjoy studies unless I can see a practical purpose. The thought of college doesn't appeal to me although I did like the interior design class and the drafting class. I'm not sure why I even thought to take those classes. Maybe in a past life, I was building the pyramids. I think that would be what Edgar Cayce would say. Anyway, I have a plan for a life with Katherine so that takes care of that. I don't care what we do or where we go as long as we are together.

Thanksgiving is fast approaching, and Annie invited us to spend the weekend with her. She invited Dr. Sharon for Thanksgiving dinner also. Dr. Sharon said she would pay for the purchase of the turkey and fixings, or rather my father would be paying. Katherine's sister was easily persuaded to let Katherine stay with us instead of spending the money to get her back to Michigan. Anyway, her parents would not be returning home until the 10th of December.

A week before Thanksgiving, there was a special announcement over the PA system by Sister Joseph. Her announcements always started with "Girrrrrls!" We intuitively knew something was coming that would not be good news.

"It has come to my attention that there is a perverse club in town called *The Beat*. It is a den of iniquity that no good Sacred Heart young lady should take part in. If any of our girls are found to be attending any of these beatnik perversions, you will be expelled immediately. Remember who you are representing at all times. Thank you."

Of course, we were going. Funny thing is, we probably wouldn't have even heard of the place if Sister hadn't told us about it. We had heard of beatniks, but no one had ever seen one or knew exactly what went on in one of these coffee houses. We did know that there was an image to uphold consisting of a black turtleneck sweater, black jeans, black glasses, bongos and possibly a black beret. As we discussed this Beat Generation philosophy together, we pieced together enough vital information for our successful integration.

We spent the week diligently researching every detail of this project. Katherine wrote a song. We can either sing it or recite it as a poem. Janette can play the bongos to accompany it, Katherine will play the guitar, and I will snap my fingers and whisper words in the background. Cool! Thank God, Katherine had over-packed and has two pairs of slightly different black jeans, plus two black turtleneck tops. One is cotton and the other is wool. She even has a beret.

Thanksgiving Day we congregate in Annie's kitchen. We are five women cooking and singing together. We are all allowed to drink wine while we work. Is it the heat from the oven and stove or the wine that gives us the rosy glow to our cheeks?

Dr. Sharon and Katherine do not know how to cook, but they are great little sous chefs. I find excuses to check on their progress so I can pat Katherine on the ass and blow in her ear. She finds ways to reciprocate. I don't think we are fooling any-one, but it is way more provocative sneaking a feel.

After the food is prepared, and in the oven, the kitchen is cleaned and the table is set, Janette says, "Hey, let's do our act for mom and Sharon. I'll go get the bongos from downstairs."

Katherine says, "I'll get my guitar. You two get comfy. Lo, come with me."

We have just enough time to kiss. "I love you, Katy bear." I hold her close and she slides my hand up her sweater. To my delight, she is not wearing a bra. The feel of her breast in my hand fills me with desire. "I'm getting wet." I lift her sweater and fondle her nipple with my tongue. She groans and pushes my head into her breast.

We hear Janette come up the basement stairs. Katherine grabs her guitar and we make a beeline for the living room. I can feel the heat still on my face.

Somehow, we pull it together and perform our act perfectly. I don't know if it's the wine or my hormones, but I think, "Holy shit, this could actually work." Annie and Sharon clap enthusiastically and yell "Bravo." I guess they couldn't very well throw tomatoes, but still, it felt good.

Dinner is delicious and the conversation stimulating. It is especially interesting because Sharon is participating for the first time. We cover some of the same old subjects we always like to mull over: religion and politics. She is pretty well-versed in all the different philosophies and is surprisingly liberal considering that she is part of the older establishment.

After dinner, Janette's boyfriend, Larry, shows up for pie. We all snuggle into the living room to watch a special on TV. Sharon falls asleep in a chair. Katherine and I lay on the floor. Annie turns the lights off so the only light in the room is from the TV. We are all sleepy from the turkey and wine, and soon Annie is asleep also. Larry and Janette slip away into her bedroom. Katherine and I give each other knowing looks and fall asleep looking into each other's eyes.

Around ten, Larry and Janette sneak back in and announce, "It's time for pie." I recognize the flush in her cheeks.

After pie, the party is over and guests go home. Katherine is relegated to the sofa and Janette and I go to her room. We each have a twin bed. We review the day in the dark and agree it was one to remember.

41

Beatniks and Bongos

The next day we rehearse all day. Annie knows what the plan is and wants to go with us.

"I can look like a Beatnik," she pleads. We ask her to drop us off and then come in separately so we don't look like we are with our mom. But by the time we are all dressed and ready to go, she looks like she is in her early 20's – not at all like a mom.

We enter the front entrance with trepidation, not knowing what to expect. It is dim, with little lights on each of the many small tables. It's hard to really see anyone at first until our eyes get accustomed to the dark, but then we see three Juniors from school sitting in the corner. We spot each other and nod in collusion.

We sit at a table in the middle of the room but only a couple of tables from the stage. The waitress arrives and we are not sure what to order, so we ask her what she recommends. There is regular coffee, something called espresso, and soft drinks. She apologizes for having no liquor available until they get their liquor license and then adds, "Of course, if we did serve liquor we would have to card." We get the message. Katherine takes the lead by ordering espresso and Janette says, "Make it three." When the waitress leaves, we both look at Katherine and ask, "What is espresso?"

"I don't know, but it sounds more interesting than coffee or a Coke." We agree. After all, this is an adventure.

When our waitress returns with three small cups of a very dark liquid and a sugar dispenser, we ask who we need to talk to in order to perform. She looks at Katherine's guitar case and the bongos and replies with a condescending smirk, "You'll just judge the right time and go."

We can see that there are bongos on the stage, and we felt embarrassed that we brought our own, but Janette says "Fuck those bongos. I like mine." And that gives us back a little confidence. *Yeah, fuck those bongos, and fuck that waitress. What a cunt,* I think to myself. I realize I swear a lot when I'm stressed. What would Martina say?

The espresso requires a lot of sugar. Otherwise, it would be undrinkable. We don't really like it at all, but as the place fills up, we order more to justify our existence.

Finally, a guy gets up and moves to the small platform of a stage. He moves the stool out of the way and tests the mic. It's not much of a sound system, but it's not much of a room to even require a sound system. It seems like overkill, but then again it looks professional. He opens a notepad and begins to read his poetry.

I don't get any of it, but I clap when he steps down. This may be inappropriate. A few people are snapping their fingers in approval, and one other person claps with me. I think it's probably Annie. Most just sit quietly. I guess they are pondering his deep message. Yeah, right.

A couple of other guys get up and recite some psychobabble. What a joke. No one takes the stage and we don't make a move for it either. We are pinned to our chairs.

Then surprise, surprise, Annie comes through the tables, up on the stage and pulls the stool up to the mic. I am wide-eyed and holding my breath. Janette whispers "Oh crud."

Annie sits and looks out into the audience, building the suspense. Then she says "A Koan." She pauses and lets the word sink in . "Question. What is the Buddha? Answer. Three pounds of flax." Silence. Then she continues.
"Because it is so very clear,
it takes longer to come to the realization.
If you know at once the candlelight is fire,
The meal has long been cooked. A Koan."

As she leaves the stage, the room is silent and then it erupts in snapping fingers. I've never heard such a sweet sound. She walks past us and winks and smiles.

"I don't think we can follow that," I say, even though I have no idea what it meant.

"No, we have to. She did it for us. Let's go." Katherine grabs her guitar and we follow like lemmings. She stands at the mic and pushes the stool over to Janette. Janette sits and puts her bongo between her legs, waiting for the cue. I stand just to the left of Katherine.

She begins to sing slowly but with a beat that we have practiced. I'm so nervous I can't remember anything, but my body remembers the repetition.

And when her body boldly found me, suddenly the night surrounds me. I repeat. (Surrounds me)

As the breadth and depth of her love astounds me. (Astounds me)

Was there ever such a night? The magic still I can't believe. (Can't believe)

That I could hold and breathe such love, I hardly can conceive (Hardly conceive)

When I feel her love long gone the pain surrenders to her

light (Her light)

As I remember how she gave to me, her breath of life that night (That night)

When we finish, we stand there frozen, not knowing how to leave. We never rehearsed that part. Then from the back of the room, Annie stands and yells "Bravo" and claps wildly. The room follows her declaration of enthusiasm. I try to contain my joy. Inside, my body wants to jump up and down and scream with all my might.

Instead, we move as one, back to our table like it's just another night, but we are forever transformed. We are broken free from our chrysalis and born again.

In the car on the way home, we are all laughing and talking at once. We are high on sugar, caffeine, and life. Annie is smiling like a Cheshire cat.

"What made you get up and do a koan? Was it your plan all along?" I ask.

"Not at all, but when I saw you three stuck to your seats and not making a move, I decided I would do something to set the bar low to give you courage. I had no idea they would like it."

"And instead you raised the bar."

"Well, you rose to it. Aren't you happy it went that way instead of following a bunch of low bar guys?"

"Yes, it worked out perfectly, but Katherine was the one who saw what you did and made the move, or else we would still be sitting there." Katherine and Annie are our inspiration. Neither one tries to deny her gifts. They are both good receivers and that is another lesson they teach in their humble way.

On Monday when we return to school, we see the three Juniors in the lunchroom. They pass our table and smile and snap their fingers. Cool! Two weeks later *The Beat* closes its doors. There is an editorial in the paper that Janette brings us. In short, it says that Coffee Houses and Beatniks are for the big cities where there is a wealth of talent. It is true and that is why we are headed to New York.

42

The Day That Music Died

December 16, 1960, will be etched in my brain forever. At lunch, Janette says, "I have something to tell you. I hope you won't be mad at me."

"What? We promise we won't get mad," I reassure her.

"Okay, well, um, I guess there isn't any way to say it other than, I'm pregnant."

"Oh no! I mean, yikes, how did that happen? I mean, now what?" I'm not sure if I should look happy or alarmed. I'm certainly not happy because this really ruins our whole plan, unless . . . .. Well I don't even know if there are choices. Katherine is unusually quiet.

"Larry and I are getting married over Christmas break. I won't be able to come back to school here so I will probably finish at Central High and at least get my diploma. That's what mom wants me to do, but I think why bother? What do you think?"

"Gosh, Janette, are you really in love? I mean this is a big step. Are you ready to have a kid and be a housewife? Is this what Larry wants?"

"Yeah, Larry says we should get married. I was thinking I should have the baby and give it up for adoption, but he says he loves me, and he doesn't want to give his baby away."

"Hey, it's not up to Larry. Larry's life will go on with little interruption, but yours will be all but done. You could give it up and then we could still go on with the plan after you give birth. We can wait for you. What do you think, Katherine?"

"I think Janette has to do what she wants and what feels is right for her. Don't think about us, or Larry or even what your mom wants. This has given me a headache. I know what I would do, but you gotta do you." Katherine says this as she is getting up to leave the table. She has a frown on her face and is rubbing her temples.

"What would you do? Tell me, Katherine." Janette pleads.

"I'll tell you tomorrow. Meanwhile, pray on it. Search your heart."

The bell rings and we go to our classes in a daze. At 2:00 we meet for PE. Today is volleyball. I love the game. Finally, something physical to release some pent-up energy.

Katherine says she has a headache so she gets a pass. She sits on the floor leaning up against the wall and watches me. It makes me perform and try all the harder for her enjoyment.

The score is all tied up with only five minutes to go. A serve comes right at me and I do a jump and slam dunk that scores what I hope is the winning point. I look over at Katherine and give her a big smile. She smiles and gives me a thumbs up. Then she rolls her eyes and makes a face and falls over on her side.

I think "You nut. You are so cute." But then her body stiffens, and I can't take my eyes off her. What is she doing? My teammates yell at me as the ball flies past my head.

Then I see white foam forming in the corners of Katherine's mouth. Like an idiot, I am paralyzed trying to make sense of it until it hits me, and I can hear myself screaming.

I run to her pushing girls out of my way. I slip my hands

underneath her and hold her head in my arms trying to lift her up.

"Help! Help! Help! No, No, No!" Her eyes are rolled back into her head, the foam keeps coming from her mouth. I can hear myself as if in a dream. This can't be real. This isn't happening.

I get pushed out of the way as adults swarm around her. I fight to stay but we are all pushed farther away. I can't see anything that is happening. The ambulance arrives and she is put on a stretcher and taken away. I am frantic with fear. Janette is by my side holding on to me and crying. I am not crying. What is there to cry about? This is not real. This is a joke.

"Shhhhh." I hear Janette saying "Shhhhh, there, there." Now I hear myself shouting, "No, no, no, no, no, no, no, no."

At 3:00 the bell rings and day students descend the doors of Sacred Heart to meet up with each other at burger joints or load into cars and plan for their Friday night and weekend events. Many are oblivious to the horror that has occurred. The news would spread like wildfire now. Would it ruin anyone's weekend? After all, she was just a boarder that no one really knew. It didn't happen to them.

I stagger out with Janette to Larry's car. We sit in silence after Larry is informed of the news. There are no words, only questions. It is little comfort to be together, but it is better than being alone.

A song on the car radio is interrupted by a news flash. A United Air Lines DC-8 bound for LaGuardia Airport in New York collided with TWA L1044 Super Constellation. One plane crashed over Staten Island and the other over Park Slope, Brooklyn, killing all 128 people on both airplanes and six people on the ground. It is the highest death toll in commercial aviation history. A Catholic high school teacher, from St. Augustine High School less than two blocks from the crash, reported seeing the faces of the DC-8 pilots as the plane approached the school, and that the wing dipped to clear the school building just before the plane crashed. A student at the school, who lived in one of the destroyed apartment buildings on the block of the crash site, reported that his entire family was in the only room of their apartment not destroyed by the crash and thus survived.

I don't know what to think. I don't want to think, so I start doing math in my head. Today is $1+2+1+6+1+9+6 = 26 = 2 + 6 = 8$. What does 8 mean? Think, think, does it mean anything? Should I have gleaned anything if I would have looked it up this morning? Could I have stopped this? What did I do wrong? There are 361 days left in the year. $3+6+1=9$. Nine is the number of Completion.

Around 4:00, it's dark already and we are cold still sitting in the car. Larry starts the car and runs the heater, but I can't stay here forever. They can't stay here. Annie will be expecting Janette to be home by now.

"Would you have Annie call Dr. Sharon and tell her what we know. Ask if she can get any more information for us? Can I come to your house tomorrow?"

"Of course. We'll pick you up as usual. Will you be all right tonight?" She begins to cry again. We hold on to each other unwilling to let go.

Finally, Larry says "Do you want me to walk you back to Sienna Hall?" That is our cue to release our grip.

"I'll see you tomorrow." As I get out of the car, I know the wind is freezing cold, but I don't feel anything even though I only have my blazer for protection. I am numb.

In the leisure room, I wait for news – any news, any piece of information. Karen says, "No news is good news." I want to believe her, and I do until I see Dr. Sharon come through the door. Her face says it all, but then I think *it's just her face. It's the face of an adult who has seen too much, been through too much. It's the face of bad news.*

My legs are like Jello but somehow, I get them to hold up my body and walk to her. "I'm so sorry," she says. My legs go lifeless and I begin to fall but she catches me. She and Karen drag me over to the couch.

Karen asks, "What do you know?"

Dr. Sharon says "She had a brain aneurysm. That's a blood vessel that has burst in her brain. She never regained consciousness. Her family is having her body sent back to Michigan. She is already gone."

"She's gone? Already gone? I can't see her or say goodbye. Just like that, she is gone?" I am still in shock, but I recognize the platitudes coming at me. "She's in a better place. She went fast, she didn't suffer. I know how you must feel. Blah, blah, blah."

"Shut up! Shut the fuck up. You don't know how I feel. How do you know she didn't suffer? What makes you think she's in a better place? Shut up, shut up."

I still haven't cried. My tears have turned to rage. I get up and Dr. Sharon tries to help me, but I brush her arms away. "Leave me alone. I'm going to bed."

On my way to my room, I stop at Katherine's room. I think I will sleep there tonight, but the room is filled with nuns. They have packed up her stuff. Taken everything off the walls. I have nothing. Couldn't they wait one day? It's like she never existed. Stupid, fucking nuns. Cunts, bitches.

Saturday at Janette's was probably not the thing to do, but what was the right thing to do? Nothing can help. Dr. Sharon says grief takes time and everyone is different. "Just let it move through you the best way for you. If you want to talk, we are all here for you. Or we can just be together."

Annie says, "We didn't judge when she came into our lives and we can't judge when she decided to leave. These things are written long before. We are just blessed that she was in our lives for as long as she was. We all learned something and loved her unconditionally." The others agree and say nice things about her and bring up cherished memories.

I'm not ready to talk. I'm afraid of what might come out. My anger is deep and dark. I'm angry at her for leaving; for not telling her sister about me. Or maybe she did, and if that is the truth, then I'm angry at her sister for not including me. I'm angry at the ambulance people for not saving her, at the nuns and adults that pushed me away and I'm angry at myself for not doing more, for not going with her. I should have insisted. I should have been with her. She was alone and with strangers in the end.

Sunday morning, I do not get out of bed to go to Mass. At 9:00 Sister Joseph is knocking at my door. I don't answer, but she comes in any way. I have no privacy, I have no power to keep her out.

"Loretta, I'm going to force you to get up for your own good. You should be in church praying for Katherine's soul. I just hope she didn't die with a mortal sin on her soul for there is no way out of hell. Or even a venial sin on her soul. We have to pray for her to get out of purgatory. Light candles and offer money for special Masses for her. Venial sins add up and even thoughtless chatter and immoderate laughter can build up venial sins that if not redeemed by repentance and God's forgiveness it causes exclusion from Christ's Kingdom and the eternal death of hell. Absolution cleansing can be painful in the lower levels of Purgatory and for this reason, we pray for the dead to ease the transition out. I don't know if there was a Priest there to give her the last rites, so we must pray for her every day."

I get up to shut her up. I now know what I must do. I can no longer stay in a philosophy that would condemn a beautiful child of God to hell. This place is now Hell to me. There is no God in this place.

"Yes, Sister. I will call Janette and she will pick me up and I can go to her parish for Mass. Thank you, Sister."

When Janette picks me up, I tell her I am leaving. "I have to get out of here. Would Annie loan me the train fare? I will send you the money as soon as I get home."

"I'm sure she will, but are you sure you need to go? We will all miss you so much." Janette gets misty again.

"I know. I'll miss you too, but you'll be leaving school and I won't see you that much anyway. I just can't stay there any longer. Sister Joseph said Katherine is either in Hell or Purgatory if she even had a venial sin on her soul. How mean is that?"

"Oh, crud. Yeah, you have to leave. Let's go get you some money."

43

Elvis has Left the Building

Thankfully you don't have to wait too long for a train leaving for Chicago. I figured I had until five o'clock before Sister Joseph or Dr. Sharon came looking for me and by that time I'd be long gone. Annie and Janette said they would cover for me by saying they dropped me off at the movie after church and that I said I would take the bus back to school. If the cops were called in, then they would say that I was talking about going back home, but they didn't think it was today. I'm sure the old man would be alerted and not give a shit.

On the long journey home, I have a lot of time to contemplate. I try to make sense of the senseless. What is this thing we call life? Is life long, like T.S. Elliot says in *The Hollow Man* or is it short like Katherine's? Is it suffering like the Buddha said or is it a bowl of cherries or a piece of cake? Is it a blessing? Or do we all take up the cross when we come here? Is it our destiny? Our karma?

"Out, out brief candle." Is life nothing more than an illusion? Is the world a stage and we are merely players? "Like a poor actor who struts and worries for his hour on the stage, and then is never heard from again." Did Shakespeare have it right?

Is life what you make it? Is it a choice? Are we here to serve as Sister Diane proclaims and is God watching our every move? Waiting for us to fuck up and then judge us? Are we here to learn and evolve? Are we making it up as we go with our thoughts? Thoughts are things. What was Katherine thinking? Is this all just an accident? Is everything just random? The luck of the draw? Is life a story told by an idiot, full of sound and fury but devoid of meaning? Shakespeare's words blend with mine from involuntary memorization.

Here we are, held on earth by gravity while we are spinning around the sun at over 1,000 miles per hour and at the same time rotating every 24 hours. We don't even realize any of this or that we are on this blue ball seemingly floating in space. What if we are somebody's pet project, like an ant farm? We scurry around thinking we are making progress when actually none of this matters. Are we just making up stories to keep ourselves from freaking out?

I don't have answers. No, actually I do. I don't believe in anything. I know I will never love anyone again. It's too dangerous. Whether it's my karma that makes them leave me, or if it's my lesson or my cross to bear, I cannot bring someone else into it. We both will lose.

It seems like an eternity since I was in Rockton. The cabbie asks me where to? I ask him to take me through downtown. It's five o'clock and there seems to be more traffic than I remember. The streets are decorated with the same old fake green garlands hanging across the streets from one light post to another and a cheap gold star in the middle. Bedraggled though the decorations are, they still bring a tug of nostalgia to my heart. Why? I can only guess because of the times I spent with Sandy and the Boxers or with Miss Sarah. I can still feel her hand through my mitten as we stood looking at the window displays in Choate's Department Store.

The two theatres are still there, but the ticket booths are

empty right now. The marquee on one says Elmer Gantry and across the street is playing Psycho. I see Arnie's Bar is open for business. There has to be one bar open for God's sakes and I imagine he is doing a pretty good business. Nothing like Christmas to make you want to get drunk.

Thinking of drunks, I wonder if "you know who" is in there getting his nightly drunk on? I am going to give this one more try, and if he insults me one more time I'll just clean out his stash of cash hidden in the upper shelf of his closet and see if I can hook up with Martina.

"What are the biggest changes you've seen here in the last two years?" I ask the cabbie.

"Um, maybe more tract homes," he says

"What is a tract home?"

"Prefab on a slab." He lets it go at that and I don't try to force any further conversation. When we get to my house, I give him a generous tip and wish him a Merry Christmas.

The house is dark and the porch light is not on, but I can still see that it needs a coat of paint. The path to the door is piled with snow. There is a light layer of crystallized ice on top. I wonder how the old man traverses this terrain when he is stinking drunk. I hear the crunch of each step as I carefully make my way to the front porch steps. The screen door is partly frozen shut or just warped with neglect. It looks like someone has swept the steps recently. Otherwise, the simple act of opening the screen door could be hazardous to life and limb.

Pulling open the door, I step into the kitchen. This is the only door we ever used to enter the house. It's not the front door but it's the door closest to the driveway and garage. My fingers easily find the light switch out of habit. The light goes on over the kitchen table. I scan the room for old familiar landscapes and anything new. Everything is the same as it was two years ago when I left.

I remove my wet shoes, take off my coat and hang it over a kitchen chair. I inhale deeply and smell the odor of a house not lived in, not loved or cared for. For a couple of seconds, I see it transformed into the design I had created in school. I wonder if he would let me do it. I wonder if I would have the courage to ask?

Right now, all I care about it retreating to my Elvis sanctuary. I want you; I need you; I love you. There is the same squeaky fourth step and I count the steps as I always have – 12, 13, 14 to the top of the landing. Turn right, six steps to my bedroom door. Am I the only one who counts things like this?

I open the door and my fingers flip the switch. I blink and blink again. Is this another mirage? NO! Nonononnnnooooo. There is no Elvis. There are no familiar well-loved furnishings and books or record player or any of my collected valuables. The room is painted barf green. The closet is empty. Do I exist? Did I ever live here? What the fuck! Oh, of course, I get it. He thinks he has erased me. I'm just a crazy nightmare that was but is no more.

44

Come to Jesus

Okay, Old Man, let's get this on. We're having a come to Jesus tonight.

Methodically, I search the house. First, find the stash. It's still there and there are eighteen one-hundred-dollar bills. Second, I retrieve the gun from on top of the cupboards. Climb! Yes, Motherfucker, I will climb. Third, I call the 24-hour drive-thru liquor store. "Hi, I need a fifth of Jack and a carton of Lucky's delivered."

"I'm sorry lady, we don't deliver. We're a drive-thru."

"Well, Honey, I have a hundred-dollar tip that says you do."

There is a short silence. "What's the address?"

Fourth, I go looking in the basement for any signs of my old life. There are unmarked boxes and an inspirational can of barf green paint. I'll look in the boxes later. Right now, I have some painting of my own to do.

I have the kitchen door open as I paint my masterpiece so I can see the delivery guy when he drives up. *Merry Xmas, Motherfucker!* Loretta, you're a regular Picasso, and nothing says Christmas like something in green.

A car pulls in, and I see a young entrepreneur with a bottle of Jack and a carton of Lucky's slip-sliding his way up the path. I meet him at the steps.

"Thanks for making it so fast. Hey, do you have matches?" I hold out two one-hundred-dollar bills. "Keep the change."

"Thanks, lady! Here keep it." He hands me his Zippo.

"Merry Christmas" I proclaim as he drives out of sight. "And to all a good night."

Okay, back to work, but first a nice big drink. The clinking of ice cubes in my glass sounds so festive. The first swallow burns and I gasp for breath, but the next one goes down smooth and cool as jazz.

We should have some music for this party. I turn the knob and the radio blasts Bobby Helm singing *Jingle Bell Rock* and I sing along while I find my favorite butcher knife. Jingle bell, jingle bell, jingle bell rock! Oh, how invigorating to sing while I hack away at the couch where the old man did his dirty deeds. I slash the couch to shreds and move on to his mattress. I avenge my mother and Katherine and all women who have been betrayed by life.

"The poison of deep grief, it springs from her father's death." I think that is how Shakespeare said it, but I'm not sure or even why this quote pops into my head. It's not my father's death I grieve, but Katherine's. But then again, he is dead to me now. There is no more try or hope. But before I go, I will get the apology, the confession and the truth that I need before absolution can be granted. The big WHY?

Exhausted from my tirade, I retreat to the kitchen chair and pour another two fingers of Jack. I have delayed the gratification of a Lucky Strike, but now I engage my Zippo to perform its duty. The end of the cigarette burns bright red as I inhale, deeply filling my lungs with the sweet nicotine rush of smoke. It burns my lungs and makes my head buzz with a dizzy glee. I like the burn even though I have a coughing fit. It makes me feel alive. The blurry clock on the wall is either ten or eleven.

No, it must be ten or maybe nine. Well, who gives a fuck? It's "kiss my ass goodbye cocksucker" o'clock. Ha, ha! Loretta you still got it.

The headlights roam the kitchen walls as he turns into the driveway. The porch light is on so he can see my Christmas greeting painted on the door. My excited heart is beating loudly with adrenalin and nicotine. The screen door creaks and slams shut. Heavy footsteps come toward me and stop.

"Goddamn it! Son of a bitch! You little cunt!" He's playing his top three hits.

Daddy's home! The kitchen door swings open hard, crashes into the wall and bounces back hitting him in the shoulder.

"Welcome home, Asshole." I stare into his malevolent bloodshot eyes, and he stares into mine. Quickly he sees the bottle of Jack, the cereal bowl overflowing with cigarette butts and the butcher knife on the table in front of me.

"I want you out of here now. You are not welcome in my home. Get your fat ass up and get out." He slurs some of his words and weaves back and forth.

"Oh, I never was welcome in this house, but I'm not leaving yet. First, we are going to clear the air, you and me. Sit *your* fat ass down and get uncomfortable."

"I suppose you think you're going to make me with that knife?" He sneers and gives a snort.

"No. I think I'm going to make you with this." I take the gun from my lap and point it at him. "Now sit your ass down."

I hadn't actually planned on threatening him with it. I only wanted the gun to protect myself if he tried anything, but now I see his fear and I like it.

He looks around as if hoping for reinforcements, and in his search, he spies the couch.

"Jesus Christ, Loretta, what have you done?" I think it might be dawning on him that I am a crazy bitch, and I am capable of shooting his ass.

"It's not what I've done you worthless piece of shit. We are talking about what you have done. Now sit down." I shove the bottle towards him. "Have a drink. You're gonna need it."

Finally, he sits. He looks at the bottle and hesitates. He's not sure what to do. "Go ahead, have a drink. I insist."

He reaches for the bottle, but his eyes never leave mine even as he takes a swig. He clears his throat. "Look Loretta." His voice is condescending now.

"Hey, shut up. I'll tell you when you can talk. I love what you've done with my room. Was it fun for you? Did you think you were never going to see your crazy daughter again? Was it cathartic? Did you cum?"

He starts to say something, but I cut him off. "Shut up, Moron. Don't you know you are not supposed to speak unless given permission? Jesus, you're dumb."

He is starting to sweat even though the door is still standing open and the temperature is quickly dropping in the kitchen. He takes another swig from the bottle and removes his coat.

"Now back to your remodeling job. Did you get some perverse pleasure knowing you were destroying something that I loved? Maybe the only thing here that meant anything to me? Did you sit up nights thinking of what shitty thing you could do next to punish me for killing your wife? That's it, isn't it? You blame me for her death."

He doesn't respond. He knows it's useless to try to defend himself because it's true. He cannot ameliorate our history.

"Okay, I'm just going to tell you that what you did to my room was the last straw. It literally broke me and now you have to pay. You have to pay for all the things you took away, you have to pay for all the names you called me, for the mental abuse, and for all the physical abuse, you motherfucker, or should I say 'daughter-fucker'?"

His face is getting red. I see the blue vein in his neck expand in anger. He shouts "You wanted it. You asked for it. And big deal it only happened a few times. I wouldn't fuck you again with somebody else's dick." The last two drinks kick in and give him the balls to defend himself.

"I was eight!" We are both shouting now. "How could I ask for it? You want to blame everybody for your sins. How about *you* killed my mother? You fucked her and that's why she died. A grown ass man blames his eight-year-old daughter because he put his cock inside her. That's a story for the police. Maybe it's time to confess before you go to jail? Do you want to tell the police what you did or should I just shoot your cock off instead? I think you should get on your knees and pray for forgiveness. Go ahead, get on your knees."

His face is suddenly drained of blood. "I'm sorry." He clutches his chest. "Loretta, call the operator. I need an ambulance. Help." His voice is weak and wimpy.

"I'm not calling shit and neither are you. You need my help? Ha, I wouldn't piss on you if you were on fire." Watching him grimace in pain was a real Christmas gift, but I had seen this act and I was not going to fall for it again. I let my guard down before and he took my weakness and shoved it up my ass.

"I'm waiting. Say you're sorry and pretty please with sugar on it."

He pushes himself out of his chair and almost falls over with it.

"Don't even think about touching that phone." I watch with suspicion as he staggers outside. He doesn't get very far when he falls to the ground. I wait a minute expecting him to get up, but he doesn't move. My thoughts are panicky as I think, "Oh shit, maybe he isn't faking this time." I better cover my ass just in case.

"Operator, can you call an ambulance. I think my daddy has had a heart attack. He's fallen in the yard. The address is 513 S. 8th St."

I hear the siren as I'm rushing to hide the gun, the knife, the Jack. Nothing I can do about the door except turn off the porch light so no one sees it. The siren is close now. I see the flashing lights so I run outside to meet it and wave my arms wildly. Should I be over by him? What would a loving daughter be doing right now?

The cold air and the adrenalin have sobered me up, or at least I think I am acting like I'm sober, but I am probably babbling. They jump from the ambulance and are all on the old man.

The driver comes to me and asks "Is this your father? Where is your mother?"

"Yes. She's dead."

45

His Hour Upon the Stage

Within minutes of their arrival, the old man is lifted on a stretcher and hauled into the back of the ambulance. The driver says, "Come, ride with me." He helps me into the seat beside him and away we go.

"What's your name?" he shouts over the siren.

"Loretta."

"I'm Dan. What happened?"

"I don't know. All of a sudden, he just grabbed his chest and ran out the door and then dropped. Is he dead?"

"They are working on him. Don't worry, he is in good hands."

The only sound now is the ominous wail of the siren screaming through the streets.

At the hospital, Dan leads me into the Emergency waiting room and tells me to sit. He goes to the nurse on duty and talks and points to me. When he is finished, he comes back and says, "Just wait here and they will take care of you and let you know what is happening with your dad." He pats me on the shoulder and asks if I need him to stay. I shake my head no.

The nurse arrives with a warm bath sheet. It feels like it just came out of the oven. She wraps it around my shoulders, and I realize I'm shivering from the cold and I left my coat back in the kitchen. The blanket feels very comforting and I am so grateful.

She hands me a pen and some paperwork to fill out, but she says to take my time and she will be back. When she returns, she has a cup of tea. "Here, drink this. It will warm you up." I don't like tea, but I drink it on demand.

She sees that I have not made an attempt to fill out the paperwork and she asks, "Would you like for me to help you with the paperwork?"

I say, "Yes, please." I just want someone with me. I feel like an infant, incapable of doing anything without help. When the paperwork is finished, she asks if I need anything else.

"I really have to pee. Where is the john?" On the toilet, all the scenes replay in my head – over and over without resolution. What is the conclusion? Did I make this happen? I didn't intend for this to happen, or did I? Did all my affirmations of "I hate you and I hope you die" make this come true? If I did, I'm sorry. I don't want him to die. I'm not angry at him anymore. I just want peace. Did I kill my mother and my father? I throw up in the sink.

At 2:34 a.m., I am told he has passed. They did all they could. Where do I want the body sent? Can they call anyone for me? Do I want a priest?

When I get back to the house, I am exhausted and already suffering from a hangover. But, before I can sleep and before anyone sees my artwork, I know I must paint the porch door green. I do finally sleep, but it is more of a wakeful sleep. I'm probably sleeping but I think I am awake. I give up and get up at 7:00 a.m.

Priorities: Pee and then drink about a gallon of water, pee some more. Drink coffee and smoke a cigarette. By the second cup of coffee and the third cigarette, I feel the spark of life coming back into my body. Then I see the bag of his belongings that the nurse gave me at the ER, and the memories start their re-runs. Diversion, that's what I need so I begin to invade his privacy. There are the clothes he was wearing and his shoes and belt. I picture him naked. I wonder why they stripped him down. Then there is a small bag that proves to be much more revealing

First, I find his Timex wristwatch. Timex takes a licking and keeps on ticking. A fifty-cent piece, two quarters, a dime and several pennies, and a wallet. I look in the wallet for money. There are nine one-hundred-dollar bills and a twenty.

I flip through the identification cards, and then there it is. A picture of me smiling back. It looks like a high school graduation picture. Oh my God, it's my mother. I've never seen a picture of her, but it must be her because otherwise it's me and it's not me. I stare at it until my eyes water. She is beautiful. She has light brown hair and good skin, but those are the only differences between us. I pull it out and look on the back. She has autographed it, "My Darling Robert, Your Lovey."

I don't know how to process this information. Our striking resemblance has so many implications. It's like a puzzle and here is a missing piece, but the rest of the pieces are now lost forever.

Maybe that's all right because I can make up the rest of it for a fairytale ending. I feel lighter now just knowing that she existed and she looked like me and she was beautiful. I slow dance and twirl around the kitchen, holding her picture in the air. She was real and she loved me.

I gather his clothes in the bag and add his coat to the bundle so I can burn all of it. I feel his truck keys in one pocket along with a comb and a checkbook. I thumb through and find the balance. There is $50,000 in his personal checking account? I think I might be rich.

I see he has written many checks to Sacred Heart. In fact, so many that I think I should have a wing named after me. There are many more to Dr. Sharon and fifty dollars a month to someone called Gloria Hansen.

I spend the rest of the day working on my plan A and plan B. Plan A: I am stinking rich and all my dreams come true. Plan B: I'm rich enough and I'll work to get to plan A.

46

Lawyers, Men and Money

Monday morning, I walk into the office. Jeff looks up in surprise.

"Hey, Loretta. Long time no see. Merry Christmas."

"Yeah, Merry Christmas Jeff. I have some bad news. My father passed away. He had a heart attack."

"Oh no! I'm, I'm so sorry." I can imagine the confusion going through his head right now.

"Here's what I want you to do. Tell Luke to come to my office. Do not tell him why. Bring me the books and the job log."

I walk into my father's office. I mean, my office. Jeff is hesitating, and I think about giving him a kick in the ass in case there is any doubt who is the boss, but instead, I wait to see if he responds to my orders. He does.

I begin to investigate the contents of the desk, but before I get too far Luke arrives and Jeff follows with a set of books and some job orders. "Thanks, Jeff."

I get up to meet Luke. He is all smiles and I give him a big hug. "You is all grown up, Gal. Look atchu."

"Sit down Luke." His face loses his smile. I sit behind the desk and fold my arms and put on my sad face. "He's gone, Luke. He had a heart attack and died. I know it's a shock for all of us, but we must go on. I will need your help, but we can get through this."

"I will do whatever I can, Miss Loretta. I'm so sorry. He was a good man. Um, ah, is you planin to sell?" I see now that he is worried about his future and I see that this is my strong suit.

"No, Luke. I'm taking over. I have been taking courses to be ready for this. I just didn't think it would happen so soon. For the last two years, he has been preparing me to come into the business with him. I will miss his guidance, but I know that I can count on you now."

He nods in agreement, so I continue.

"If there is any one of your guys that you think you need to replace, now is the time. Give me their names tonight after work. Bring all the guys to my office with you and I will tell them about my father's passing and how we will all work together now. I'm going to give everyone time off with pay through the New Year, so finish any projects you are working on now. If there are any projects scheduled after that, I will call them and reschedule." I hand him the worksheets, and he shuffles through them.

"We be finished up by tomorra an' the rest can wait."

He gets up and I reach across the desk to shake his hand. "Thank you, Luke. I know I can count on you."

The books tell the story. The story of a cheap-ass bastard multi-millionaire. Plan A goes into effect.

"Jeff? Get me Max Bergman on the line." My father's attorney assures me I inherited everything and since there is no will, he will handle it quickly through probate. The wheels of the judicial system in Rockton have been greased for many years by Nelson Concrete. You may not be able to buy love, but you can buy everything else.

"I'll be back after lunch, Jeff. Please have the payroll finished to the end of the year. Did my father give Christmas bonuses?"

"Yes, he gave us $50."

"Give everyone a $100 bonus and give Luke and yourself $500." Loyalty is for sale also.

"Wow, thank you, Miss Nelson. Thank you so much."

I consider telling him to call me Loretta, but on second thought Miss Nelson suits me just fine.

I'm off to shop for some clothes since I have an empty closet. I'll choose tailored slacks and blazers with white cotton shirts. It's the closest thing to a man's suit for work.

It's after two o'clock when I return to the office. I have picked up poinsettias and gift certificates for turkeys at Piggly Wiggly for all employees. I'm driving the old man's truck, so I have Jeff unload the plants. The truck reeks with the stench of old man and booze. I'll ask Luke if he wants it.

When Jeff finishes unloading the plants, I ask him to write an obituary. "I'm too emotional to do it. Would you mind doing it for me? And then run it over to the Register." It's good to be the boss.

At 3:30, he brings it to me to edit. I pretend to read it, but truly I could give a shit. "Good job. Thank you, Jeff. You can use the truck if you want. The keys are in it."

As soon as he steps out the door, the phone rings. I look at it like it's a foreign object. Snap to it girl, you're the boss. "Nelson Concrete."

"Yes, um, hello. This is Mr. Bosch from Bosch…"

"Yes, Mr. Bosch, this is Loretta Nelson."

"Oh, I just wanted to clarify that there will be a wake tomorrow night and Wednesday evening from 6 to 9 if that is good for you."

"Let's cancel tomorrow and just go with Wednesday night."

"One other thing Miss, what would you like your father to be dressed in?"

I search my brain. I burned what he was he wearing last night. I guess that wouldn't be right anyway. "I'll bring over his favorite suit tonight. Okay?"

"And you did wish to have him cremated?"

"Yes, that's right, Mr. Bosch. His wishes, not mine. Oh, I forgot to put the service information in the obituary I just wrote and sent over to the Register. Would you mind terribly calling and adding to that?"

"Of course. I'll call right now. Thank you."

"No, thank you, Mr. Bosch." There is a lot of thanking going on and I don't know why I'm thanking him. He should be thanking me for all the money this is costing. That reminds me, there must be an insurance policy somewhere.

Jeff returns around four o'clock. "I have to run home and get something, but I'll be right back. If Luke comes back and has any names of guys he wants to let go, you can make a check out for an additional two-week's severance. Leave it on my desk."

I rush to the house and look through his closet for something suitable for a funeral. There isn't much to choose from so that makes it simple.

When I get back to the office, Luke is there and Jeff asks to talk to me. "Whatever you have to say, you can say in front of Luke. What is it?"

"It's just that one of the two people he wants to let go is the Foreman. Are you sure you want that to happen?" He doesn't look at Luke.

"What about it, Luke? Are you sure you want to let him go?"

"Yez, I is sure. I should be the Foreman. I knows more and I be here longer. Only cuz he be white, thaz all." He looks down at his feet. I must teach him to use eye contact.

"And who is the other person you are letting go?" I ask.

"Juz sum fool frien of his. Lazy, too."

"Okay. Done and done, but you need to do something for me if you want to be the Foreman."

"What eva yu say."

"Jeff, would you run this suit over to Bosch Funeral Home? You can take your check and leave me your phone number in case I have any questions, but otherwise, I'll see you next year. Oh, and leave me a couple of signed checks in case I need to buy something for the company in your absence."

When Jeff leaves, I ask Luke to come into my office. "Luke, we need to be completely honest with each other. Now, I respect you and I know you can be an excellent Foreman, but I need you to clean up your speech. Your diction needs to be impeccable if you want the customers to respect and trust you. Do you understand what I'm saying?"

"Yez, Miss, I sho does."

"Okay, right there is a problem. It's pronounced yes and . . ." Oh, screw it. I was originally going to make him go to night school, but I think the whole family could use it.

"Luke, I'm going to hire a tutor to come to your house. Okay? I mean, you aren't offended, are you?"

"No, Miz Loretta." I can tell he would like to say more but shit, he's self-conscious now. I feel slightly guilty but if there is one thing I learned from Martina, it's that speech is a key to success. I try to take the pressure off by asking about the girls and Tyrone.

"They fine. Tyrone's in the Army. Girls is good and Sarah sure be happy you is back." He is actually trying now. Taking his time and thinking as he speaks. Progress already.

Clyde, the Foreman, doesn't handle being let go without a fight. I tried to pin it on the weather. Business slows down in the winter and who knows what will happen to the company without my father.

"You're not the only one I have to let go, but you'll be the first one I will call when things pick up." That seemed to calm him down. Denial and hope are a wonderful human trait.

The other guys are all happy with time off with pay and a bonus. Even Clyde calmed down with the money, the plant and the Piggly Wiggly turkey.

It's six o'clock and I should be exhausted. I've been going strong for twenty-four hours, but instead, I wish there were ten more hours to go. I make a to-do list for tomorrow.

- Call Rockton Ford and order a new truck.
- Find a contractor to renovate the kitchen.
- Find the insurance policy.
- Send Annie a thousand dollars.
- Go through all the job orders.
- Go through all the books.
- Hire a tutor.
- Call Sister Joseph and have her ship all my things. Be nice.
- Get a driver's license.

I drive home in the stinking truck and finally, I have a pizza delivered. I have forgotten to eat today. I have smoked two packs of Lucky's. Around nine o'clock I collapse on my bed and I don't wake up until noon.

On Wednesday, I continue to work on my to-do list until five o'clock and then I dress in my new gabardine slacks and black blazer. I stop for something to eat even though I'm not hungry. It's just a way to postpone the inevitable.

Ford has delivered a new red Ranchero to my door. Money is power and I am wielding all my new power in every direction, but I still have to do things I don't want to do. Nobody wants to go to a wake or a funeral.

I arrive at the funeral home ten minutes to six. Mr. Bosch meets me at the front door with his best undertaker face. I almost want to laugh.

"Miss Nelson, come this way." He leads me to a rather large room where I see the casket surrounded by a shit load of flowers and theatrical lighting.

"I will close the doors and give you private time to be with your loved one," he says. The viewing of the corpse is one of the fundamentals of the economy of the funeral industry.

I approach the casket with trepidation, and I scan his body for any signs of life. They have painted his face so he looks very healthy – robust even. He's all dressed up and no place to go. They have placed him in a very comfy looking casket and he is positioned in a peaceful repose. It's creepy. I wonder if he sees this farce from somewhere above – or more likely below. As a businessman, would he appreciate the requirement of a viewing that constitutes the bulk of the funeral costs?

I'm more interested in who all these flowers are from. I don't recognize many of the names, but I can tell they are all business associates. Every important name is there from the mayor, the sheriff, several judges and other government officials, including the Governor. Really? I gotta hand it to him. He knew what to kiss and when. As Katherine would say "There's a lesson."

A deep sadness overwhelms me again. It's the first time I've thought of Katherine since the train ride. I begin to cry, and it's hard to stop even when I hear voices outside the door. I know I have to go out there.

When I open the door, a line of people are looking at me. I'm glad I look like I've been crying for him as a daughter should.

The line moves slowly as each person stops to offer their condolences, and surprisingly, most are telling me stories of my father's generosity and how he helped in a time of need. The image of a pillar of the community, a humanitarian, a visionary, a philanthropist, and a "really swell guy" who will be missed is something I can only imagine. I shake my head in agreement like I knew this person they are talking about and I thank them for telling me and coming tonight.

When Miss Sarah and Luke show up, the floodgate of tears reopens. She tells me that they were the only family in their area that had a septic tank, an indoor toilet, and a shower – all because he had it installed for them. The shower makes me think of Tyrone. I begin to sob and Miss Sarah hugs me, and that makes it impossible to stop.

I just remember Katherine saying, "There is so much good in the worst of us and so much bad in the best of us, that we really can't judge." I cry for the deep loss. I feel for her. I cry for me and for the "swell guy" I never knew.

Miss Sarah releases me and I see that there is a long line building behind her. Ruthie and Marilee are there, and I can't believe how grown up they are. Ruthie is pregnant and little Marilee is graduating from high school next year. Of course, Tyrone isn't there, but the other boys are and we hug like old friends.

Jeff is patiently waiting for the line to end to ask me if there is anything I need him to do.

"No, I'm ok."

He gives me a hug and then he says, "I was told to throw these away, but I saved them for you anyway." He hands me a packet of letters addressed to me in care of Nelson Concrete. They are from Sandy. Tears streaming down my cheeks like Niagara Falls, I clutch the letters to my chest and thank him profusely.

I make a dash for the john so I can do the ugly cry and get it all out. So many emotions to deal with all at the same time. "When sorrows come, they come not in single spies but in battalions." Shakespeare again.

I get up the strength to emerge once more and hope all the people have left and I can go home. I don't get too far when I almost physically bump into Margaret. It reminds me of the time at the Goodwill store.

We are both unprepared for the sudden meeting. She speaks first but I don't hear what she has said to me because I am focused on the child holding her hand. Auburn hair and familiar blue eyes stare back at me. It is a smile that would beguile most humans, but not the green-eyed monster rising in me. She is wearing a navy-blue velveteen coat with a white rabbit fur collar and a muff to match. It's an outfit I would have sold my soul for at that age. It's not rational but I hate her.

I look away and listen to Margaret speaking condolences that don't ring true. We face each other feeling our way around our awkward past.

"Thanks for coming, Margaret. I don't think this is anything for a kid to see, but again thanks for the thought."

She reaches out to touch my arm. Does she feel the flinch in my muscle?

I turn my attention to the room and pretend I'm needed there so I must take my leave.

"Oh, just one minute, please, Loretta. I have something important to tell you – privately." She points to the bathroom door. "Bobbi, go ahead and go to the bathroom."

The kid hesitates for a second and Margaret gives her a push. Her black rubber galoshes squeak as she skips to the bathroom door. There is a small puddle of melted snow where she was standing. I'm fixated on it.

"Okay, what?"

"Well, I guess there is no easy way to say this, so I'll just come out with it. Bobbi is your sister. Robert has been paying support money every month since she was born an . . .."

I cut her off. "Get out. Get out!" I say between clenched teeth. "I can't believe what a selfish bitch you are. This is so wrong on so many levels, and you drag this kid here to tell me this bullshit, at my father's funeral? You are a liar Margaret, and a whore." I walk away as fast as I can without running.

47

Fake It Til You Make It

At home, I can feel the release of the stress I've been holding in my neck and shoulders. I try to breathe through the stiffness and let it go. I pour myself a Jack and Ginger Ale and light a cigarette before I open the letters from Sandy. I open the latest one first and notice that she is now spelling her name with an 'i' instead of a 'y'.

Dear Lolo, I am making one last attempt to express myself. I'm thinking with my heart, not my head, to recall the many memories we've shared. Secrets, jokes, and "someday dreams" we shared with only each other.

You've seen me at my best and sometimes at my worst. We would laugh so hard we would wet our pants and tears would run down our faces. We would have each other to survive through heartaches. We would go to so many movies and always be the "Star!" We could be whoever we wanted to be.

We would sit on your porch floor – legs apart – and play jacks for hours. As the years went by, we both vowed we would always keep in touch. What happened?

Thank you, Lolo for all the memories, all the laughs, all the surprises, best-laid plans, and all the love you gave me.

No matter what, YOU are my "dear sister, Lolo"
Love All-ways,
Sandi

I spend Christmas with the Johnson's. It is bliss. I lavish gifts on my forever family. I surprise Miss Sarah with the first of many powder puff blue Cadillacs. A Family is all I have ever wanted for Christmas. What more could I ask for?

I have my family; I am rich; I am the boss. I am the granter of all wishes to those I love and those who loyally serve me. I have Sandi back in my life. I have a semi-famous best friend who could be my ticket to meeting Elvis.

Sister Diane was right. God does work in mysterious ways. All the times when I was floundering or treading water, trying not to drown, now it seems like there always was a plan.

I must forgive my father so that I can be free, but it won't come easily. He gets a free pass and his unblemished reputation only grows, while I cannot tell anyone about his dirty secrets. Who would believe me anyway? Plus, I can't jeopardize my new business with the truth, so I will bury my anger like the nightgown in the alley.

I could feel sorry that he only saw the loss and not the gain. He crushed the flower and kept the thorns. It could have been so different, but the past is over, and I see the lesson for me is to let go of the loss and relish the gain. Learn from his mistakes.

Of course, there is still the child who has my father's eyes, but just like Scarlet O'Hara, I will think about that tomorrow. For now, I have my family to take care of, my Tara to remodel, and a business to run.

There is a part of me that is in fear – fear that I might run his business into the ground. After all, what do I know about concrete or management or schmoozing politicians? I might be making history as the girl who is worth a *small* fortune. The joke being that I started with a *large* fortune. But then again, Eleanor Roosevelt said, "The Future belongs to those who believe in the beauty of their dreams."

I know I'm a survivor. Now, I am also The Boss. Sandi reminded me that I can be the Star in my own movie. And from now on, I am going to be the architect of my own life. I just hope it works.

Acknowledgments

Carolyne Ruck: My editor. Without her, there would be no book. Always smiling, always encouraging, always with the best advice. I can't thank her enough.

Caren Cantrell: Editor, writer, pure genius. Pulled all the loose ends together and made me look good. Kudos!

John Bizal: English teacher extraordinaire, non-judgmental, generous supporter. Bridge cohort and Jeopardy winner. He is the only reason I began to write this book and rewrite this book.

Sylvia Clements: BFF, life coach, Wonderwoman. Everyone should have her as a mentor. She should write a book.

Peggy Finley: Smartest woman in the room. Always willing to help and share. Beautiful inside and out. I trust her with my life, my money, and my secrets. Sister code. PIC, BFF.

Jake Decker: Cover designer, artist extraordinaire who went above and beyond to ensure the cover captured the feel of the book.

About the Author

So Much Bad in the Best of Us is the debut novel from author Cheryl Robillard.

Born in Winona, Minnesota she lived with her grandparents until the age of eight, when her mother and her new step-father moved her to central Illinois. There she attended Sacred Heart, a Catholic high school. Coming of age in the late '50s gave Cheryl first-hand experience of what it meant to be a teenager at a time when things were changing in America. Rock and roll redefined the music scene and the beatnik movement gave credence to creative expression. The women's movement and the sexual revolution had not yet begun. *So Much Bad in the Best of Us* draws on that experience, rocketing us back to a time that was perhaps not as innocent as it appears by today's standards.

After a successful career in sales, Cheryl switched her focus to the metaphysical and became an ordained minister, working with Hospice. She also creates unique art that she sells through her company Ditzy Glitzy. The idea for this novel had been percolating for several years but it wasn't until she joined a book club that she finally got up the courage to put pen to paper.

Cheryl lives in sunny Scottsdale, Arizona with her beloved cat, Bob.

Made in the USA
San Bernardino, CA
27 March 2019